THE PELICAN SHAKESPEARE

GENERAL EDITOR ALFRED HARBAGE

MUCH ADO ABOUT NOTHING

WILLIAM SHAKESPEARE

MUCH ADO ABOUT NOTHING

EDITED BY JOSEPHINE WATERS BENNETT

PENGUIN BOOKS

Penguin Books
625 Madison Avenue
New York, New York 10022

First published in *The Pelican Shakespeare* 1958
This revised edition first published 1971
Reprinted 1973, 1974, 1978

Library of Congress catalog card number: 75-98356

Printed in the United States of America by
Kingsport Press, Inc., Kingsport, Tennessee
Set in Monotype Ehrhardt and Linotype Times Roman

CONTENTS

PUBLISHER'S NOTE

Soon after the thirty-eight volumes forming *The Pelican Shake-speare* had been published, they were brought together in *The Complete Pelican Shakespeare*. The editorial revisions and new textual features are explained in detail in the General Editor's Preface to the one-volume edition. They have all been incorporated in the present volume. The following should be mentioned in particular:

The lines are not numbered in arbitrary units. Instead all lines are numbered which contain a word, phrase, or allusion explained in the glossarial notes. In the occasional instances where there is a long stretch of unannotated text, certain lines are numbered in italics to serve the conventional reference purpose.

The intrusive and often inaccurate place-headings inserted by early editors are omitted (as is becoming standard practise), but for the convenience of those who miss them, an indication of locale now appears as first item in the annotation of each scene.

In the interest of both elegance and utility, each speech-prefix is set in a separate line when the speaker's lines are in verse, except when these words form the second half of a pentameter line. Thus the verse form of the speech is kept visually intact, and turned-over lines are avoided. What is printed as verse and what is printed as prose has, in general, the authority of the original texts. Departures from the original texts in this regard have only the authority of editorial tradition and the judgment of the Pelican editors; and, in a few instances, are admittedly arbitrary.

SHAKESPEARE AND
HIS STAGE

William Shakespeare was christened in Holy Trinity Church, Stratford-upon-Avon, April 26, 1564. His birth is traditionally assigned to April 23. He was the eldest of four boys and two girls who survived infancy in the family of John Shakespeare, glover and trader of Henley Street, and his wife Mary Arden, daughter of a small landowner of Wilmcote. In 1568 John was elected Bailiff (equivalent to Mayor) of Stratford, having already filled the minor municipal offices. The town maintained for the sons of the burgesses a free school, taught by a university graduate and offering preparation in Latin sufficient for university entrance; its early registers are lost, but there can be little doubt that Shakespeare received the formal part of his education in this school.

On November 27, 1582, a license was issued for the marriage of William Shakespeare (aged eighteen) and Ann Hathaway (aged twenty-six), and on May 26, 1583, their child Susanna was christened in Holy Trinity Church. The inference that the marriage was forced upon the youth is natural but not inevitable; betrothal was legally binding at the time, and was sometimes regarded as conferring conjugal rights. Two additional children of the marriage, the twins Hamnet and Judith, were christened on February 2, 1585. Meanwhile the prosperity of the elder Shakespeares had declined, and William was impelled to seek a career outside Stratford.

The tradition that he spent some time as a country

teacher is old but unverifiable. Because of the absence of records his early twenties are called the "lost years," and only one thing about them is certain – that at least some of these years were spent in winning a place in the acting profession. He may have begun as a provincial trouper, but by 1592 he was established in London and prominent enough to be attacked. In a pamphlet of that year, *Groats-worth of Wit*, the ailing Robert Greene complained of the neglect which university writers like himself had suffered from actors, one of whom was daring to set up as a playwright :

. . . an vpstart Crow, beautified with our feathers, that with his *Tygers hart wrapt in a Players hyde*, supposes he is as well able to bombast out a blanke verse as the best of you: and beeing an absolute *Iohannes fac totum*, is in his owne conceit the onely Shake-scene in a countrey.

The pun on his name, and the parody of his line "O tiger's heart wrapped in a woman's hide" (*3 Henry VI*), pointed clearly to Shakespeare. Some of his admirers protested, and Henry Chettle, the editor of Greene's pamphlet, saw fit to apologize :

. . . I am as sory as if the originall fault had beene my fault, because my selfe haue seene his demeanor no lesse ciuill than he excelent in the qualitie he professes : Besides, diuers of worship haue reported his vprightnes of dealing, which argues his honesty, and his facetious grace in writting, that approoues his Art. (Prefatory epistle, *Kind-Harts Dreame*)

The plague closed the London theatres for many months in 1592–94, denying the actors their livelihood. To this period belong Shakespeare's two narrative poems, *Venus and Adonis* and *The Rape of Lucrece*, both dedicated to the Earl of Southampton. No doubt the poet was rewarded with a gift of money as usual in such cases, but he did no further dedicating and we have no reliable information on whether Southampton, or anyone else, became his regular patron. His sonnets, first mentioned in 1598 and published without his consent in 1609, are intimate without being

8

explicitly autobiographical. They seem to commemorate the poet's friendship with an idealized youth, rivalry with a more favored poet, and love affair with a dark mistress; and his bitterness when the mistress betrays him in conjunction with the friend; but it is difficult to decide precisely what the "story" is, impossible to decide whether it is fictional or true. The true distinction of the sonnets, at least of those not purely conventional, rests in the universality of the thoughts and moods they express, and in their poignancy and beauty.

In 1594 was formed the theatrical company known until 1603 as the Lord Chamberlain's men, thereafter as the King's men. Its original membership included, besides Shakespeare, the beloved clown Will Kempe and the famous actor Richard Burbage. The company acted in various London theatres and even toured the provinces, but it is chiefly associated in our minds with the Globe Theatre built on the south bank of the Thames in 1599. Shakespeare was an actor and joint owner of this company (and its Globe) through the remainder of his creative years. His plays, written at the average rate of two a year, together with Burbage's acting won it its place of leadership among the London companies.

Individual plays began to appear in print, in editions both honest and piratical, and the publishers became increasingly aware of the value of Shakespeare's name on the title pages. As early as 1598 he was hailed as the leading English dramatist in the *Palladis Tamia* of Francis Meres:

As *Plautus* and *Seneca* are accounted the best for Comedy and Tragedy among the Latines, so *Shakespeare* among the English is the most excellent in both kinds for the stage: for Comedy, witnes his *Gentlemen of Verona*, his *Errors*, his *Loue labors lost*, his *Loue labours wonne* [at one time in print but no longer extant, at least under this title], his *Midsummers night dream*, & his *Merchant of Venice*; for Tragedy, his *Richard the 2*, *Richard the 3*, *Henry the 4*, *King Iohn*, *Titus Andronicus*, and his *Romeo and Iuliet*.

9

The note is valuable both in indicating Shakespeare's prestige and in helping us to establish a chronology. In the second half of his writing career, history plays gave place to the great tragedies; and farces and light comedies gave place to the problem plays and symbolic romances. In 1623, seven years after his death, his former fellow-actors, John Heminge and Henry Condell, cooperated with a group of London printers in bringing out his plays in collected form. The volume is generally known as the First Folio.

Shakespeare had never severed his relations with Stratford. His wife and children may sometimes have shared his London lodgings, but their home was Stratford. His son Hamnet was buried there in 1596, and his daughters Susanna and Judith were married there in 1607 and 1616 respectively. (His father, for whom he had secured a coat of arms and thus the privilege of writing himself gentleman, died in 1601, his mother in 1608.) His considerable earnings in London, as actor-sharer, part owner of the Globe, and playwright, were invested chiefly in Stratford property. In 1597 he purchased for £60 New Place, one of the two most imposing residences in the town. A number of other business transactions, as well as minor episodes in his career, have left documentary records. By 1611 he was in a position to retire, and he seems gradually to have withdrawn from theatrical activity in order to live in Stratford. In March, 1616, he made a will, leaving token bequests to Burbage, Heminge, and Condell, but the bulk of his estate to his family. The most famous feature of the will, the bequest of the second-best bed to his wife, reveals nothing about Shakespeare's marriage; the quaintness of the provision seems commonplace to those familiar with ancient testaments. Shakespeare died April 23, 1616, and was buried in the Stratford church where he had been christened. Within seven years a monument was erected to his memory on the north wall of the chancel. Its portrait bust and the Droeshout engraving on the title page of the First Folio provide the only likenesses with an established claim to authenticity. The best verbal vignette was written by his rival Ben Jonson, the more impressive for being imbedded in a context mainly critical:

... I loved the man, and doe honour his memory (on this side idolatry) as much as any. Hee was indeed honest, and of an open and free nature: had an excellent Phantsie, brave notions, and gentle expressions.... (*Timber or Discoveries,* ca. 1623–30)

*

The reader of Shakespeare's plays is aided by a general knowledge of the way in which they were staged. The King's men acquired a roofed and artificially lighted theatre only toward the close of Shakespeare's career, and then only for winter use. Nearly all his plays were designed for performance in such structures as the Globe – a three-tiered amphitheatre with a large rectangular platform extending to the center of its yard. The plays were staged by daylight, by large casts brilliantly costumed, but with only a minimum of properties, without scenery, and quite possibly without intermissions. There was a rear stage gallery for action "above," and a curtained rear recess for "discoveries" and other special effects, but by far the major portion of any play was enacted upon the projecting platform, with episode following episode in swift succession, and with shifts of time and place signaled the audience only by the momentary clearing of the stage between the episodes. Information about the identity of the characters and, when necessary, about the time and place of the action was incorporated in the dialogue. No place-headings have been inserted in the present editions; these are apt to obscure the original fluidity of structure, with the emphasis upon action and speech rather than scenic background. (Indications of place are supplied in the footnotes.) The acting, including that of the youthful apprentices to the profession who performed the parts of women, was highly skillful, with a premium placed upon grace of gesture and beauty of diction. The audiences, a cross section of the general public, commonly numbered a thousand, sometimes more than two thousand. Judged by the type of plays they applauded, these audiences were not only large but also perceptive.

THE TEXTS OF THE PLAYS

About half of Shakespeare's plays appeared in print for the first time in the folio volume of 1623. The others had been published individually, usually in quarto volumes, during his lifetime or in the six years following his death. The copy used by the printers of the quartos varied greatly in merit, sometimes representing Shakespeare's true text, sometimes only a debased version of that text. The copy used by the printers of the folio also varied in merit, but was chosen with care. Since it consisted of the best available manuscripts, or the more acceptable quartos (although frequently in editions other than the first), or of quartos corrected by reference to manuscripts, we have good or reasonably good texts of most of the thirty-seven plays.

In the present series, the plays have been newly edited from quarto or folio texts, depending, when a choice offered, upon which is now regarded by bibliographical specialists as the more authoritative. The ideal has been to reproduce the chosen texts with as few alterations as possible, beyond occasional relineation, expansion of abbreviations, and modernization of punctuation and spelling. Emendation is held to a minimum, and such material as has been added, in the way of stage directions and lines supplied by an alternative text, has been enclosed in square brackets.

None of the plays printed in Shakespeare's lifetime were divided into acts and scenes, and the inference is that the author's own manuscripts were not so divided. In the folio collection, some of the plays remained undivided, some were divided into acts, and some were divided into acts and scenes. During the eighteenth century all of the plays were divided into acts and scenes, and in the Cambridge edition of the mid-nineteenth century, from which the influential Globe text derived, this division was more or less regularized and the lines were numbered. Many useful works of reference employ the act–scene–line apparatus thus established.

Since this act–scene division is obviously convenient, but is of very dubious authority so far as Shakespeare's own structural principles are concerned, or the original manner of staging his plays, a problem is presented to modern editors. In the present series the act–scene division is retained marginally, and may be viewed as a reference aid like the line numbering. A star marks the points of division when these points have been determined by a cleared stage indicating a shift of time and place in the action of the play, or when no harm results from the editorial assumption that there is such a shift. However, at those points where the established division is clearly misleading – that is, where continuous action has been split up into separate "scenes" – the star is omitted and the distortion corrected. This mechanical expedient seemed the best means of combining utility and accuracy.

THE GENERAL EDITOR

INTRODUCTION

Much Ado about Nothing is a feast of wit from the senten-
tious rhetoric of Leonato's opening lines to Benedick's last
pun. There is abundant variety from the delicious uncon-
scious humor of Dogberry's anxiety to be "writ down an
ass" to the delicate counterpoint of sentiment and semblance in Claudio's penance, when he is made to do ob-
sequies to an empty tomb. Among the consciously witty
characters Beatrice and Benedick easily carry off the prize,
not so much because they have more wit than the others as
because they are so sympathetically and so fully human-
ized. Shakespeare's acute observation of their kind of
love-making has provided a pattern for the greatest English
comedies from *The Way of the World* to *The Importance of
Being Earnest*, yet Beatrice and Benedick have never been
surpassed. It takes a very great actress, however, to convey
the full womanly charm of Beatrice ; to read her lines with
spontaneity but without pertness, to make her Beatrice the
warmhearted and not Katherine the shrew. As Ellen Terry
has said, her lines "should be spoken with the lightest
raillery, with mirth in voice and a charm in manner"
which keeps her vivacious but never shrill.

The *Stationers' Register* confirms the internal evidence
that this play was written when the poet was at the height
of his skill in comedy. It was in the hands of the printer by
August 4, 1600, along with *As You Like It*, *Henry V*, and
Jonson's *Every Man in His Humor*, when all were "staied"

from publication. But on August 23 the license for this play was granted, and it appeared before the end of the year. How long before August, 1600, it had been written is not clear; but it is not mentioned in the well-known list of Shakespeare's comedies in Francis Meres' *Palladis Tamia* (1598), and it is therefore usually dated 1598–1600, probably coming between *As You Like It* and *Twelfth Night*.

Unlike Rosalind and Viola, the heroines of these companion comedies, Beatrice does not protect herself by donning men's clothing. Her self-defense, we might say her disguise, is her wit; and her unmasking is not physical but psychological. She betrays in her very first words that self-conscious and intense interest in Benedick which is characteristic of young love. Modesty and propriety cannot keep her from breaking into the conversation of her elders to inquire whether "Signior Mountanto returned from the wars or no." She must be reassured that he is safe, yet she is too self-conscious to say his name. Her cousin understands her, however, and Beatrice plunges deeper into her self-betrayal in an effort to cover up her interest and yet to learn more about Benedick. "But how many hath he killed?" "Who is his companion now?" These are the questions that torment the woman in love: where is he? what is he doing? who is his companion? Beatrice's disparagement only emphasizes the fact that she can think of nothing else. Yet her wit is her protection, the disguise which conceals her true feelings, even from herself.

It keeps Benedick at sparring distance, although he thinks that she exceeds Hero in beauty "as the first of May doth the last of December." His fear of her tongue and his habitual pose as a confirmed bachelor protect him doubly until the trick played upon him by the Prince, Claudio, and Leonato throws down both barriers at once. They were not very formidable barriers. His defiance of Cupid in the first scene is not only ominous, but it betrays a certain vulnerability. Claudio's defection from the fraternity of bachelors has its effect, and Benedick is already thinking what kind of woman he could love before he is persuaded that Beatrice loves him.

Even after each is convinced of the other's love, however, they cannot break through the barrier of persiflage until the emotion aroused by Hero's disgrace beats down their self-conscious reserve. Benedick blurts out his "I do love nothing in the world so well as you" almost involuntarily, and Beatrice is trembling on the verge of the same confession, though she keeps her guard up until she is sure that he is serious. She never for a moment forgets Hero, however. Her confession is prefaced by "I am sorry for my cousin," and when she has put Benedick on the defensive, so that he offers to prove his love, she responds instantly, "Kill Claudio." This is a very feminine seizing of an emotional advantage, but it does credit to her heart and head that she never wavers in her loyalty to her cousin, nor does she forget Hero's predicament in the excitement of her own confession of love. Her "O that I were a man" rings with womanly rage and frustration and forces Benedick to take up a responsible role in the vindication of Hero. In this scene we are shown the depth and honesty of Beatrice's character. Her earlier consternation when she overhears Hero and Ursula discussing her, and her quick decision to reform, expressed in joyful lyric, are no more than we might expect from the evidence of her interest in Benedick; but her steadfast loyalty to her cousin strikes a deeper note and a sweeter one. She will rule Benedick by her wit taking advantage of his love, but he has wit enough to be proud of her and do willing service. Once they have confessed, the revelation of the trick played upon them is, of course, something they can jest about and end with a kiss. They were not tricked into falling in love but only into the realization that they were in love.

The Hero–Claudio story must be regarded as the main plot because of its melodramatic and spectacular character, yet Shakespeare carefully keeps us from entering into the emotions of either Hero or Claudio. This he does by the title he gives the play, by the selection of a familiar story whose happy outcome was familiar to his audience, by his handling of the characters of Hero and Claudio, and finally by his manipulation of the plot so that we know even before Hero is denounced that the Watch have all the evidence necessary to clear her.

The title of the play is not, as is sometimes claimed, evidence of Shakespeare's indifference, but is his careful reassurance that the gravest events of the play will have no serious consequence. The story of the maiden falsely accused was a very old one, going back to post-classical romance. It was widely known because it had been retold by two very popular writers, Ariosto in the *Orlando Furioso* and Bandello in his *Novelle*. Ariosto's version was translated into English by Sir John Harington (1591), and it had been retold by Peter Beverley as the *Historie of Ariodanto and Ieneura* (1566) and by Spenser in the *Faerie Queene* (1590). Richard Mulcaster had presented a play before the Queen in 1583, *A Historie of Ariodante and Geneuora*. Bandello's version was known in England both in the original Italian and in the French of Belleforest's *Histoires Tragiques* (1576). The names and some elements in the plot indicate that Shakespeare knew both versions.

Considering the popularity of the story, and its theatrical qualities, it is not unreasonable to suppose that our poet knew some older dramatization, but a few mistakes in the stage directions and loose ends in the plot are insufficient to support the hypothesis that Shakespeare was making over an old play. The quarto and folio texts begin with the stage direction, "Enter Leonato Gouernour of Messina, Innogen his wife," etc., and at the opening of Act II they have, "Enter Leonato, his brother, his wife, Hero his daughter, and Beatrice his niece, and a kinsman." Yet Innogen (out of Bandello) has no part in the play. The "kinsman" also fails to appear and instead we have Margaret and Ursula. In I, ii we learn that Antonio has a son, and the son appears briefly to arrange the music, yet in V, i, 277 Claudio is told that Antonio's pretended daughter (Hero in disguise) "alone is heir to both of us." In the opening scene the messenger reports that he has already delivered letters to Claudio's uncle "here in Messina," yet the uncle is not mentioned again and is not used as explanation of Claudio's presence in Messina, as we might expect. However curious, these are all slight inconsistencies such as might very well survive from Shakespeare's own first draft.

In any case the Hero–Claudio story was a familiar one and the poet assumes his audience's familiarity with it. Modern critics have complained about the sketchy way in which he handles the deception of the Prince and Claudio and the evidence which exposed it. No less a scholar than Professor Boas objects to the omission of the "momentous episode outside Hero's chamber window." Instead we have the much more dramatic repudiation scene, the true crux of the plot. In Bandello's story the lover sends word to Leonato that he refuses to marry the girl because of her unchastity. The messenger denounces her to her father and mother, she faints and is pronounced dead, but revives, and her father, who is convinced of her innocence, conceals her in the country, etc. Shakespeare has economized on and heightened the climax by making the lover do his own accusing, and making the occasion the wedding scene. On the other hand he substitutes for the deception episode Borachio's boasting account of what actually happened. We are told beforehand of the plot against Hero's honor, and we hear Borachio boast of the sum he has been paid for deceiving the Prince and Claudio, and we see the Watch overhearing Borachio and arresting him. We have all the essentials of the deception without the scene itself. Such a scene could not be shown because it would either deceive and so confuse the audience, or it would fail to deceive the audience and so make the Prince and Claudio look too gullible.

The plot against Hero (and Claudio) is adequately presented but its melodramatic character is minimized not
only by the title of the play and the management of the
action so that Borachio is apprehended even before Hero
is accused, but also by the characterization. Both Hero
and Claudio are conventionalized so as to reduce our
emotional involvement in their distresses. Hero is a very
correct young lady and Claudio is a very proper wooer.
Hero shows not a speck of interest in Claudio until Don
Pedro hands her over to him. She is wooed by proxy and
flaunts her permission to say "yes" before Don Pedro has
had a chance to explain that it is Claudio who wants to
marry her. The nearest we come to a love scene is the
moment when Don Pedro announces the success of his
proxy wooing. Claudio makes a pretty speech and Beatrice
urges her cousin to speak, "or if you cannot, stop his
mouth with a kiss." And she interprets Hero's pantomime, "My cousin tells him in his ear that he is in her
heart." Hero herself says not a word to indicate that she is
in love. She is too proper a young lady to make choice for
herself or to do otherwise than acquiesce in the choice
made for her. She is charming, with mischief enough in
her to take part in the hoaxing of her cousin if it be "any
modest office," but she has the docility expected, and
often exacted (as in *The Taming of the Shrew*), of young
women in Shakespeare's day.

Claudio too is conventionalized. Modern performers
who romanticize the Hero–Claudio relationship by means
of stage business not called for in the lines, end by making
a perfect cad of him. He is no such thing. He is a proper
young man of his age. He sees Hero, likes her looks, and
when he has leisure he consults his superior about her.
His first question is the correct one, "Hath Leonato any
son, my lord?" Only a fool or a Romeo would rush into a
marriage without inquiring about the dowry and fortune
of the bride. Marriage was a young man's best opportunity
to get ahead in the world. Claudio is enough in love to

want to marry, but his reason is always in control of his emotions. He allows his Prince to woo for him, and Don Pedro's officiousness serves the double purpose of keeping Hero and Claudio apart and of showing us Claudio's character. He is neither furious nor jealous, as we might expect, at what appears to be Don Pedro's betrayal of his trust. He is only very sad and hurt. He blames himself and tries to be philosophical as a reasonable man should be.

This episode should prepare us for his behavior when he is made to believe that Hero is false and lewd. Nor is he too easily deceived, as some critics have said. He has seen a woman in Hero's clothes "talk with a ruffian at her chamber window"; he has heard her called "Hero"; he has heard Don John's story of her misbehavior, confirmed by Borachio. Don Pedro says that they have questioned Borachio,

> Who hath indeed, most like a liberal villain,
> Confessed the vile encounters they have had
> A thousand times in secret.

Don Pedro is perfectly convinced of Hero's guilt. How can we expect the reasonable Claudio to reject all this evidence of his eyes and ears? And being convinced, he has only one course open to him as an honorable man; he must reject her. That he does so dramatically, at the altar, indicates that he is deeply hurt and must strike back, must hurt her for having so hurt him. In this also he is seconded by the Prince.

After the altar scene, from which Claudio departs in tears, we do not see him again until the opening of the last act, where he and Don Pedro encounter Leonato and Antonio. In this tragicomic scene he speaks only three times. He reacts involuntarily to being called a "dissembler" but apologizes immediately for having laid his hand on his sword. And he asks two defensive questions, "Who wrongs him?" and "My villainy?" Not until the old men are gone and he sees Benedick can he recover his poise.

His report of the encounter, "we had liked to have had our two noses snapped off with two old men without teeth," seems unfeeling; but the spectacle of two greybeards, one of them shaking with palsy, contending which shall challenge a young soldier to a duel, has its absurd as well as its pitiful side.

The management of the audience's emotions in this scene is very adroit. It opens with Leonato's eloquent refusal to be comforted. Yet the audience knows that the Sexton is already on his way to Leonato's with the evidence which will clear Hero of scandal and Claudio of seeming a heartless dissembler. We cannot, therefore, be too deeply moved by Leonato's grief, although we sympathize with him. But in his encounter with Don Pedro and Claudio he exaggerates his grief by claiming that Hero is dead, and so reduces our sympathy. And Antonio's officious blustering dissolves the situation into comedy. Then, when Benedick in turn challenges Claudio, the scene has lost all tragic potential, and the baiting of Benedick by the Prince and Claudio leaves him looking a little foolish. Don Pedro comments, "What a pretty thing is man when he goes in his doublet and hose and leaves off his wit," to which Claudio replies, "Then is an ape a doctor to such a man." Here, as in every situation in the play, Shakespeare by keeping the audience informed of the truth (while his characters deceive each other) flatters us into a mood for laughter and effectively insulates our emotions from the distresses of his deluded characters. Leonato's understandable indignation is toned down from a tragic to a comic level by carefully graduated stages. The scene is a clash of emotion with reason, in which if reason looks rather heartless, emotion is made to look rather childish. Both are put in the wrong, and therefore in a position to be reconciled as soon as Dogberry, with Borachio in tow, arrives.

Claudio behaves throughout as the Elizabethan moralists and physicians advised. Andrew Borde, in his *Breviarie of Health* (1547), gives the standard advice in early and brief form: "First I do advise every person not to set to the heart what another doth set at the heel, let no man set his love so far, but what he may withdraw it betime, and muse not, but use mirth and merry company, and be wise and not foolish" (ch. 174). But the correct young man whose reason is always in control of his emotions does not engage our sympathies very deeply. Nor is the wrong done to Hero the betrayal of love and trust, but only the sullying of her reputation and breaking off of a desirable marriage – wrongs which can be easily and thoroughly righted.

By using a familiar story with a happy ending, and by keeping our emotional involvement with Hero and Claudio to a minimum, Shakespeare has so lightened a melodramatic plot as to make it serve as background and occasion for the warmly human courtship of the witty Beatrice and the wayward Benedick. He has brought the two love affairs to contrasting climaxes in the same scene, using the rejection of Hero as emotional preparation for the breaking down of reserve, defended by wit, which has separated Beatrice and Benedick. And he has further reinforced the comic spirit of the play by bringing into romantically imagined Messina an English village constable and his Watch – and what a constable! We know that Will Kempe, the famous comedian of Shakespeare's company, acted the part of Dogberry, because in the quarto edition of the play the names "Kemp" and "Cowley" appear instead of "Dogberry" and "Verges" throughout most of Act IV, scene ii. These men, honest as the skin between their brows, manage to do their duty and comprehend all vagrom men. They are merciful men who will not meddle or make with a thief, nor will they let a child cry in the night if they can wake the nurse. But for all their ineptitude of purpose, speech, and action, they manage to overhear Borachio boasting of his villainy and to arrest him. The most suspense-charged moment of the play is the scene where Dogberry's tediousness and Leonato's impatience combine to prevent the disclosure of Don John's plot before Hero goes to church. But immediately after the rejection scene the Sexton manages, in spite of Dogberry's method of examining, to unravel the whole matter. One more brief appearance when Borachio confesses to the Prince is all we are allowed of Leonato's honest neighbor. Not the least of Shakespeare's comic art is his parsimony.

It is not an accident that Shakespeare's wittiest comedy is largely in prose. Here prose is the language of wit and reason, poetry the language of emotion, sentiment, and rhetoric. The wedding scene begins in prose but rises quickly into verse as feeling mounts. However, Beatrice keeps her wits about her and speaks to her cousin in prose. When the Friar takes the situation in hand, he begins in what is printed as prose in the quarto, and reads like prose, but in the fourth line emotion and poetry take over. Indeed, prose and poetry are so subtly mingled that what is spoken seems perfectly fitted to the speaker and the occasion. We are scarcely conscious of the medium used, but only of the tensions and relaxations of the emotions aroused by the simple, carefully ordered plot. Yet the cool rhythms of prose have much to do with preserving the balance between reason and emotion which gives this play much of its sparkling brilliance. Here we can see Shakespeare manipulating, not puppets on the stage, but the emotions of his audience. He knows their stops and how to sound them from the lowest note of their heartstrings to the top of their compass. He takes the old plot of the maiden falsely accused and transforms it into the burden or accompaniment, the foil for his most spirited lovers – and the occasion for the inimitable Dogberry.

Hunter College   JOSEPHINE WATERS BENNETT

NOTE ON THE TEXT

The present edition follows closely the text of the only quarto of the play, that printed in 1600, evidently from Shakespeare's own draft. It is an excellent text despite irregularities in the speech and scene headings which are unusually numerous and may reflect indecisions and slight changes of plan during the process of composition. The names of the actors Will Kempe and Richard Cowley prefixing the speeches of Dogberry and Verges in IV, ii, indicate that the manuscript was closely related to the first stage production; however, the irregularities mentioned above would presumably have been eliminated if the manuscript had served as prompt-book. The quarto text is not divided into acts and scenes, and the text in the folio, which was printed from it, is divided into acts but not into scenes. The division supplied marginally for reference in the present edition is that of later editors, who divided the folio acts into scenes.

Below are listed all substantive departures from the quarto of 1600, with the adopted reading in italics followed by the quarto reading in roman. The need for emendation is remarkably slight, and most of the following instances involve mere normalization of stage directions and speech-prefixes. They are listed because of the theatrical interest of some of them. Most of the irregularities are repeated in the folio text of 1623, which was printed from the quarto and is of little value in forming the text. However, two of the folio stage directions have some slight theatrical interest. The folio adds to the stage direction at II, i, 74: "Maskers with a drum"; and gives as the stage direction at II, iii, 33: "Enter Prince, Leonato, Claudio, and Iacke Wilson," indicating that in some performance before 1623 the singer John Wilson played the part of Balthasar.

I, i, s.d. *Messina, Hero* Messina, Innogen his wife, Hero   8 *Pedro* Peter   180 s.d. *Enter Don Pedro* (Q adds: Iohn the Bastard)
I, ii, 3, 6, 16 *Antonio* Old   6 *event* euents   22 *Cousin* coosins   24 *skill* shill
I, iii, 29 *muzzle* mussel   42 *brother's* bothers
II, i, s.d. *brother* brother, his wife   *niece* neece, and a kinsman   2, 18, 43 *Antonio* brother   74 s.d. *Prince [Don] Pedro* prince, Pedro   *Don John* or dumb Iohn   88, 91, 93 *Bathasar* Bene   189 s.d. *Leonato* Leonato, Iohn and Borachio, and Conrade

24

292 *Pedro* Prince (thus throughout scene except l. 310 : Pedro)
II, iii, 7 s.d. *Exit* (at l. 5 in Q)   23 *an* and   33 s.d. *Enter . . . Music*
(combines two stage directions in Q : 'Enter prince, Leonato,
Claudio, Musicke' occurring here, and 'Enter Balthasar with
musicke' occurring at l. 39)   34 *Pedro* Prince (thus throughout)   63–64 *Then . . . go* (single line in Q)   86 s.d. *Exit Balthasar* (occurs after l. 85 in Q)   90 *ay!* I   107 *sit you* fit you
129 *us of* of us
III, i, 23 s.d. *Enter Beatrice* (occurs after l. 25 in Q)
III, ii, 1 *Pedro* Prince (thus throughout except at l. 48 : Bene)   25
can cannot   70 *John* Bastard (thus throughout)   84–85 *brother,
I . . . heart hath* brother (I . . . heart) hath   100 *her then* her,
then
III, iii, 10 *1. Watch* Watch 1   15, 25 *2. Watch* Watch 2   35 *1.
Watch* Watch   42 *2. Watch* Watch (thus thereafter until ll.
152ff; where 'Watch 1' and 'Watch 2' are resumed)   162–63
Never . . . us (part of preceding speech by Conrade in Q)
III, iv, 17 *in* it
III, v, 2 *Dogberry* Const. Dog (thus throughout except ll. 52, 56)
7 *Verges* Headb (thus throughout except l. 55)   9 *off* of   47 *be
suffigance* (Q adds Exit)
IV, i, 4 *Friar* Fran   27, 61, 85 *Pedro* Prince   48–49 *And . . .
Leonato* (single line in Q)   65, 109 *John* Bastard   153–56 *Hear
. . . marked* (printed as prose in Q, crowded at foot of page)
IV, ii, s.d. *Enter . . . Watch* (Q reads 'Enter the Constables,
Borachio, and the Towne clearke in gownes')   1 *Dogberry*
Keeper   2, 5 *Verges* Cowley   4 *Dogberry* Andrew   9 *Dog-
berry* Kemp (thus throughout except l. 61 : Constable)   35, 48
1. Watch Watch 1   43 *2. Watch* Watch 2   46 *Verges* Const   54
Watchmen Watch   62 *Verges* Couley   62–63 *hands – Conrade.
Off, coxcomb* hands of Coxcombe   67 *Conrade* Couley
V, i, 1 *Antonio* Brother (thus throughout)   96 *anticly, show* an-
tiquely and shew   97 *off* of   109 s.d. *Exeunt ambo* (occurs at l.
108 in Q)   134 *an* and   174 *on* one   198 *Dogberry* Const (thus
throughout)   244 *Verges* Con. 2
V, ii, 24–27 *The . . . deserve* (printed as prose in Q)   38 s.d. *Enter
Beatrice* (occurs at l. 39 in Q)   43 *for* (omitted in Q)
V, iii, 3 *Claudio* (appears at l. 11 in Q)   10 *dumb* dead   22 *Claudio*
Lo   22–23 *Now . . . rite* (single line in Q)   24, 30 *Pedro* Prince
V, iv, 7, 17 *Antonio* old   34 *Pedro* Prince (thus throughout except
at l. 40 : P)   54 *Antonio* Leo   97 *Benedick* Leon

MUCH ADO ABOUT
NOTHING

Don Pedro, Prince of Arragon
Don John, his bastard brother
Claudio, a young lord of Florence
Benedick, a young lord of Padua
Leonato, Governor of Messina
Antonio, an old man, his brother
Balthasar, attendant on Don Pedro
Borachio ⎱ *followers of Don John*
Conrade ⎰
Friar Francis
Dogberry, a constable
Verges, a headborough
A Sexton
A Boy
Hero, daughter to Leonato
Beatrice, niece to Leonato
Margaret ⎱ *waiting gentlewomen attending on Hero*
Ursula ⎰
Messengers, Watch, Lords, Attendants, Musicians, &c.

Scene: *Messina*]

MUCH ADO ABOUT NOTHING

Enter Leonato, Governor of Messina, Hero his daughter, and Beatrice his niece, with a Messenger.

LEONATO I learn in this letter that Don Pedro of Arragon comes this night to Messina.

MESSENGER He is very near by this. He was not three leagues off when I left him.

LEONATO How many gentlemen have you lost in this action? 5

MESSENGER But few of any sort, and none of name. 6

LEONATO A victory is twice itself when the achiever brings home full numbers. I find here that Don Pedro hath bestowed much honor on a young Florentine called Claudio.

MESSENGER Much deserved on his part, and equally re- 11
membered by Don Pedro. He hath borne himself beyond the promise of his age, doing in the figure of a lamb the feats of a lion. He hath indeed bettered expectation than you must expect of me to tell you how.

LEONATO He hath an uncle here in Messina will be very much glad of it.

MESSENGER I have already delivered him letters, and there appears much joy in him; even so much that joy could not show itself modest enough without a badge of 20
bitterness.

I, i Before the house of Leonato 5 *action* battle 6 *name* importance
11 *remembered* rewarded 20 *modest* moderate 20–21 *badge of bitterness* i.e. tears

LEONATO Did he break out into tears?

MESSENGER In great measure.

24 LEONATO A kind overflow of kindness. There are no faces truer than those that are so washed. How much better is it to weep at joy than to joy at weeping!

27 BEATRICE I pray you, is Signior Mountanto returned from the wars or no?

MESSENGER I know none of that name, lady. There was none such in the army of any sort.

LEONATO What is he that you ask for, niece?

HERO My cousin means Signior Benedick of Padua.

MESSENGER O, he's returned, and as pleasant as ever he was.

34 BEATRICE He set up his bills here in Messina and chal-
35 lenged Cupid at the flight, and my uncle's fool, reading
36 the challenge, subscribed for Cupid and challenged him
37 at the burbolt. I pray you, how many hath he killed and eaten in these wars? But how many hath he killed? For indeed I promised to eat all of his killing.

40 LEONATO Faith, niece, you tax Signior Benedick too
41 much; but he'll be meet with you, I doubt it not.

MESSENGER He hath done good service, lady, in these wars.

BEATRICE You had musty victual, and he hath holp to
44 eat it. He is a very valiant trencherman; he hath an
45 excellent stomach.

MESSENGER And a good soldier too, lady.

47 BEATRICE And a good soldier to a lady; but what is he to a lord?

MESSENGER A lord to a lord, a man to a man; stuffed with all honorable virtues.

---

24 *kind* natural   27 *Mountanto* montanto, an upright blow in fencing
34 *set up his bills* posted notices   35 *at the flight* to an archery duel   36
subscribed signed (as Cupid's representative)   37 *burbolt* birdbolt, a small
blunt arrow allowed to boys as harmless, but also Cupid's arrow   40
tax accuse   41 *meet* even   44 *trencherman* eater   45 *stomach* appetite
47 *to* in comparison with

BEATRICE It is so indeed. He is no less than a stuffed man; 51
but for the stuffing – well, we are all mortal.

LEONATO You must not, sir, mistake my niece. There is a
kind of merry war betwixt Signior Benedick and her.
They never meet but there's a skirmish of wit between
them.

BEATRICE Alas, he gets nothing by that! In our last con-
flict four of his five wits went halting off, and now is the 58
whole man governed with one; so that if he have wit
enough to keep himself warm, let him bear it for a differ- 60
ence between himself and his horse; for it is all the
wealth that he hath left to be known a reasonable
creature. Who is his companion now? He hath every
month a new sworn brother.

MESSENGER Is't possible?

BEATRICE Very easily possible. He wears his faith but as 66
the fashion of his hat; it ever changes with the next block. 67

MESSENGER I see, lady, the gentleman is not in your
books. 68

BEATRICE No. An he were, I would burn my study. But I 69
pray you, who is his companion? Is there no young
squarer now that will make a voyage with him to the 71
devil?

MESSENGER He is most in the company of the right noble
Claudio.

BEATRICE O Lord, he will hang upon him like a disease! 75
He is sooner caught than the pestilence, and the taker
runs presently mad. God help the noble Claudio! If he 77
have caught the Benedick, it will cost him a thousand
pound ere 'a be cured.

MESSENGER I will hold friends with you, lady. 80

---

51 *stuffed man* figure stuffed to look like a man   58 *five wits* mental faculties;
halting limping   60 *difference* distinguishing mark (heraldic term)   66
faith truth to his oath   67 *block* hat-block, i.e. style   68 *books* favor   69 *An*
if   71 *squarer* squarer-off, quarreller   75 *he* i.e. Benedick   77 *presently*
immediately   80 *hold* remain

BEATRICE Do, good friend.

82 LEONATO You will never run mad, niece.

BEATRICE No, not till a hot January.

MESSENGER Don Pedro is approached.

> *Enter Don Pedro, Claudio, Benedick, Balthasar, and John the Bastard.*

85 PEDRO Good Signior Leonato, are you come to meet your trouble? The fashion of the world is to avoid cost, and you encounter it.

LEONATO Never came trouble to my house in the likeness of your grace; for trouble being gone, comfort should remain; but when you depart from me, sorrow abides and happiness takes his leave.

92 PEDRO You embrace your charge too willingly. I think this is your daughter.

LEONATO Her mother hath many times told me so.

BENEDICK Were you in doubt, sir, that you asked her?

LEONATO Signior Benedick, no; for then were you a child.

97 PEDRO You have it full, Benedick. We may guess by this
98 what you are, being a man. Truly the lady fathers herself. Be happy, lady, for you are like an honorable father.

BENEDICK If Signior Leonato be her father, she would
101 not have his head on her shoulders for all Messina, as like him as she is.

BEATRICE I wonder that you will still be talking, Signior
104 Benedick. Nobody marks you.

BENEDICK What, my dear Lady Disdain! are you yet living?

BEATRICE Is it possible Disdain should die while she
107 hath such meet food to feed it as Signior Benedick?
108 Courtesy itself must convert to Disdain if you come in her presence.

---

82 *run mad* i.e. 'catch the Benedick' 85–86 *your trouble* the trouble of entertaining a noble guest 92 *charge* expense, but also responsibility 97 *have it full* are fully answered 98–99 *fathers herself* resembles and so indicates her father 101 *his head* (with its white hair and beard) 104 *marks* notices 107 *meet* suitable 108 *convert* change

BENEDICK Then is courtesy a turncoat. But it is certain I
am loved of all ladies, only you excepted ; and I would I
could find in my heart that I had not a hard heart, for
truly I love none.

BEATRICE A dear happiness to women ! They would else 114
have been troubled with a pernicious suitor. I thank
God and my cold blood, I am of your humor for that. I 116
had rather hear my dog bark at a crow than a man swear
he loves me.

BENEDICK God keep your ladyship still in that mind ! So
some gentleman or other shall scape a predestinate
scratched face.

BEATRICE Scratching could not make it worse an 'twere
such a face as yours were.

BENEDICK Well, you are a rare parrot-teacher.   124

BEATRICE A bird of my tongue is better than a beast of 125
yours.

BENEDICK I would my horse had the speed of your
tongue, and so good a continuer. But keep your way, a 127
God's name ! I have done.

BEATRICE You always end with a jade's trick. I know you 129
of old.

PEDRO That is the sum of all, Leonato. Signior Claudio 131
and Signior Benedick, my dear friend Leonato hath invited you all. I tell him we shall stay here at the least a
month, and he heartily prays some occasion may detain
us longer. I dare swear he is no hypocrite, but prays
from his heart.

LEONATO If you swear, my lord, you shall not be forsworn. 136
[to Don John] Let me bid you welcome, my lord. Being 137
reconciled to the Prince your brother, I owe you all duty.

114 *dear* great   116 *humor for that* opinion on that point   124 *rare* excep-
tional; *parrot-teacher* one who teaches a parrot by repeating monotonously
125 *A bird of my tongue* a bird that speaks   125–26 *a beast of yours* a dumb
beast   127 *continuer* one having endurance   129 *a jade's trick* i.e. dropping
out of a race just when the horse should be getting well started   131 *sum of
all* whole account (of the recent campaign?)   136 *forsworn* proved a liar
137 *Being* since you are

JOHN I thank you. I am not of many words, but I thank
you.

LEONATO Please it your grace lead on?

142 PEDRO Your hand, Leonato. We will go together.
Exeunt. Manent Benedick and Claudio.

CLAUDIO Benedick, didst thou note the daughter of Signior Leonato?

145 BENEDICK I noted her not, but I looked on her.

CLAUDIO Is she not a modest young lady?

BENEDICK Do you question me as an honest man should
do, for my simple true judgment? or would you have me
149 speak after my custom, as being a professed tyrant to
their sex?

CLAUDIO No, I pray thee speak in sober judgment.

152 BENEDICK Why, i' faith, methinks she's too low for a
high praise, too brown for a fair praise, and too little for
a great praise. Only this commendation I can afford her,
that were she other than she is, she were unhandsome,
and being no other but as she is, I do not like her.

CLAUDIO Thou thinkest I am in sport. I pray thee tell me
truly how thou lik'st her.

159 BENEDICK Would you buy her, that you enquire after
her?

CLAUDIO Can the world buy such a jewel?

161 BENEDICK Yea, and a case to put it into. But speak you
162 this with a sad brow? or do you play the flouting Jack, to
163 tell us Cupid is a good hare-finder and Vulcan a rare
164 carpenter? Come, in what key shall a man take you to go
in the song?

CLAUDIO In mine eye she is the sweetest lady that ever I
looked on.

---

142 *go together* (the Duke refuses to take precedence of his host) 145
noted noticed especially 149 *tyrant to* railer against, detractor of 152
low short 159 *buy* bid for, try to win 161 *case* i.e. clothing 162 *sad
brow* serious mind; *flouting Jack* mocking fellow 163–64 *hare-finder . . .
carpenter* (Cupid was blind, Vulcan a blacksmith) 164–65 *go in the song*
follow the tune

BENEDICK I can see yet without spectacles, and I see no such matter. There's her cousin, an she were not possessed with a fury, exceeds her as much in beauty as the first of May doth the last of December. But I hope you have no intent to turn husband, have you?

CLAUDIO I would scarce trust myself, though I had sworn the contrary, if Hero would be my wife.

BENEDICK Is't come to this? In faith, hath not the world one man but he will wear his cap with suspicion? Shall I 176 never see a bachelor of threescore again? Go to, i' faith! An thou wilt needs thrust thy neck into a yoke, wear the print of it and sigh away Sundays. Look! Don Pedro 179 is returned to seek you.

Enter Don Pedro.

PEDRO What secret hath held you here, that you followed not to Leonato's?

BENEDICK I would your grace would constrain me to tell. 183

PEDRO I charge thee on thy allegiance. 184

BENEDICK You hear, Count Claudio. I can be secret as a dumb man, I would have you think so; but, on my allegiance – mark you this – on my allegiance! he is in love. With who? Now that is your grace's part. Mark 188 how short his answer is: With Hero, Leonato's short daughter.

CLAUDIO If this were so, so were it uttered. 191

BENEDICK Like the old tale, my lord: 'It is not so, nor 192 'twas not so; but indeed, God forbid it should be so!'

CLAUDIO If my passion change not shortly, God forbid it should be otherwise.

PEDRO Amen, if you love her, for the lady is very well worthy.

---

176 *with suspicion* for fear he has grown horns, i.e. been made a cuckold by an unfaithful wife   179 *sigh away Sundays* i.e. become a good 'Sunday-citizen,' a responsible and sober married man   183 *constrain* force   184 *allegiance* loyalty to me as your prince   188 *part* speech, in the theatrical sense   191 *so were it uttered* so would he tell it   192 *old tale* (a version of the Bluebeard story in which the heroine's report of her discoveries is punctuated by these words of protest from the murderer)

198 CLAUDIO You speak this to fetch me in, my lord.

PEDRO By my troth, I speak my thought.

CLAUDIO And, in faith, my lord, I spoke mine.

201 BENEDICK And, by my two faiths and troths, my lord, I spoke mine.

CLAUDIO That I love her, I feel.

PEDRO That she is worthy, I know.

BENEDICK That I neither feel how she should be loved, nor know how she should be worthy, is the opinion that
207 fire cannot melt out of me. I will die in it at the stake.

208 PEDRO Thou wast ever an obstinate heretic in the despite of beauty.

210 CLAUDIO And never could maintain his part but in the force of his will.

BENEDICK That a woman conceived me, I thank her; that she brought me up, I likewise give her most humble
214 thanks; but that I will have a rechate winded in my fore-
215 head, or hang my bugle in an invisible baldrick, all women shall pardon me. Because I will not do them the wrong to mistrust any, I will do myself the right to trust
218 none; and the fine is (for the which I may go the finer), I will live a bachelor.

PEDRO I shall see thee, ere I die, look pale with love.

BENEDICK With anger, with sickness, or with hunger, my
222 lord, not with love. Prove that ever I lose more blood
223 with love than I will get again with drinking, pick out mine eyes with a ballad-maker's pen and hang me up at the door of a brothel house for the sign of blind Cupid.

---

198 *fetch me in* get me to confess   **201** *two faiths and troths* one to each (but also double dealing is implied)   **207** *fire . . . me* i.e. he will die at the stake for his opinion   **208** *in the despite* in showing scorn   **210-11** *maintain . . . will* win the argument except by stubborn refusal to give in   **214** *rechate* recheat, series of notes on a horn sounded to call the hounds together (with the usual reference to the cuckold's horns)   **215** *hang . . . baldrick* hang my horn on an invisible belt, i.e. be unaware of my cuckoldry   **218** *fine* finis, conclusion; *finer* more richly dressed (because spared the expense of a wife)   **222-23** *lose . . . love* (lover's sighs were supposed to consume the blood)   **223-24** *pick out . . . pen* i.e. let me be blinded by weeping over love laments

PEDRO   Well, if ever thou dost fall from this faith, thou
    wilt prove a notable argument.   227

BENEDICK   If I do, hang me in a bottle like a cat and shoot   228
    at me; and he that hits me, let him be clapped on the
    shoulder and called Adam.   230

PEDRO   Well, as time shall try.
    'In time the savage bull doth bear the yoke.'   232

BENEDICK   The savage bull may, but if ever the sensible
    Benedick bear it, pluck off the bull's horns and set them
    in my forehead, and let me be vilely painted, and in such
    great letters as they write 'Here is good horse to hire,'
    let them signify under my sign 'Here you may see
    Benedick the married man.'

CLAUDIO   If this should ever happen, thou wouldst be
    horn-mad.   240

PEDRO   Nay, if Cupid have not spent all his quiver in
    Venice, thou wilt quake for this shortly.   242

BENEDICK   I look for an earthquake too then.

PEDRO   Well, you will temporize with the hours. In the   244
    meantime, good Signior Benedick, repair to Leonato's,
    commend me to him and tell him I will not fail him at
    supper; for indeed he hath made great preparation.

BENEDICK   I have almost matter enough in me for such   248
    an embassage, and so I commit you –

CLAUDIO   To the tuition of God. From my house – if I   250
    had it –

PEDRO   The sixth of July. Your loving friend, Benedick.

BENEDICK   Nay, mock not, mock not. The body of your
    discourse is sometime guarded with fragments, and the   254
    guards are but slightly basted on neither. Ere you flout   255

227 *notable argument* famous example   **228** *bottle* basket or cage   **230**
Adam i.e. Adam Bell, a famous archer   **232** *In time . . . yoke* (proverbial)
240 *horn-mad* raving mad, also mad with jealousy   **242** *Venice* (famous for
courtesans); *quake* i.e. with fear (with pun on *quiver*)   **244** *temporize
with the hours* weaken with time   **248** *matter* sense   **250** *tuition* protection
(Claudio is imitating the formal close of a letter)   **254** *guarded* trimmed
255 *basted* lightly sewed   **255–56** *flout old ends* mock tag ends of wisdom
(or cloth)

old ends any further, examine your conscience. And so
I leave you. *Exit*.

CLAUDIO

258 My liege, your highness now may do me good.

PEDRO

My love is thine to teach. Teach it but how,
260 And thou shalt see how apt it is to learn
Any hard lesson that may do thee good.

CLAUDIO

Hath Leonato any son, my lord?

PEDRO

No child but Hero; she's his only heir.
264 Dost thou affect her, Claudio?

CLAUDIO   O my lord,
265 When you went onward on this ended action,
I looked upon her with a soldier's eye,
That liked, but had a rougher task in hand
Than to drive liking to the name of love;
269 But now I am returned and that war-thoughts
Have left their places vacant, in their rooms
Come thronging soft and delicate desires,
272 All prompting me how fair young Hero is,
Saying I liked her ere I went to wars.

PEDRO

Thou wilt be like a lover presently
275 And tire the hearer with a book of words.
If thou dost love fair Hero, cherish it,
277 And I will break with her and with her father,
And thou shalt have her. Was't not to this end
279 That thou began'st to twist so fine a story?

CLAUDIO

How sweetly you do minister to love,

258 *do me good* do me a favor   260 *apt* ready   264 *affect* aim at, desire
265 *ended action* war just ended   269 *that* because   272 *prompting* re-
minding   275 *book of words* volume of pretty speeches   277 *break with*
broach the subject to   279 *twist* (cf. 'spin a yarn')

That know love's grief by his complexion!   281
But lest my liking might too sudden seem,
I would have salved it with a longer treatise.   283

PEDRO
What need the bridge much broader than the flood?
The fairest grant is the necessity.   285
Look, what will serve is fit. 'Tis once, thou lovest,   286
And I will fit thee with the remedy.
I know we shall have revelling to-night.
I will assume thy part in some disguise
And tell fair Hero I am Claudio,
And in her bosom I'll unclasp my heart   291
And take her hearing prisoner with the force
And strong encounter of my amorous tale.
Then after to her father will I break,
And the conclusion is, she shall be thine.
In practice let us put it presently.   *Exeunt.* 296

*

Enter Leonato and an old man [Antonio], brother to   I, ii
Leonato [meeting].

LEONATO How now, brother? Where is my cousin your   1
son? Hath he provided this music?

ANTONIO He is very busy about it. But, brother, I can
tell you strange news that you yet dreamt not of.

LEONATO Are they good?

ANTONIO As the event stamps them; but they have a   6
good cover, they show well outward. The Prince and
Count Claudio, walking in a thick-pleached alley in   8
mine orchard, were thus much overheard by a man of   9

---

281 *complexion* appearance (referring to the lover's pallor)   **283** *salved*
smoothed over; *treatise* discourse   **285** *The . . . necessity* the best gift is
whatever is needed   **286** *'Tis once* it is beyond question   **291** *in her bosom*
in private to her   **296** *presently* immediately
I, ii The house of Leonato   **1** *cousin* kinsman   **6–7** *stamps . . . cover* (the
figure is of a printed book of news)   **8** *thick-pleached alley* walk lined with
thickly interwoven boughs   **9** *orchard* garden

10   mine: the Prince discovered to Claudio that he loved
      my niece your daughter and meant to acknowledge it
12   this night in a dance, and if he found her accordant, he
13   meant to take the present time by the top and instantly
      break with you of it.

LEONATO Hath the fellow any wit that told you this?

ANTONIO A good sharp fellow. I will send for him, and
      question him yourself.

18 LEONATO No, no. We will hold it as a dream till it appear
      itself; but I will acquaint my daughter withal, that she
20   may be the better prepared for an answer, if peradventure
      this be true. Go you and tell her of it.   [Exit Antonio.]
      [Enter Antonio's son with a Musician.]
      Cousin, you know what you have to do. – [to the
23   Musician] O, I cry you mercy, friend. Go you with me,
      and I will use your skill. – Good cousin, have a care this
      busy time.   Exeunt.

*

I, iii   Enter Sir John the Bastard and Conrade, his
            companion.

 1 CONRADE What the goodyear, my lord! Why are you
 2   thus out of measure sad?
 3 JOHN There is no measure in the occasion that breeds;
      therefore the sadness is without limit.

CONRADE You should hear reason.

JOHN And when I have heard it, what blessing brings it?

 7 CONRADE If not a present remedy, at least a patient suf-
      ferance.

JOHN I wonder that thou (being, as thou say'st thou art,

---

10 *discovered* disclosed   12 *accordant* agreeable   13 *take . . . top* seize the
moment   18 *appear* show   20 *peradventure* perhaps   23 *cry you mercy*
beg your pardon
I, iii The house of Leonato   1 *What the goodyear* (mild expostulation)
2 *out of measure* immoderately   3 *breeds* causes it   7 *sufferance* endurance

born under Saturn) goest about to apply a moral medi- 10
cine to a mortifying mischief. I cannot hide what I am : 11
I must be sad when I have cause, and smile at no man's
jests ; eat when I have stomach, and wait for no man's 13
leisure ; sleep when I am drowsy, and tend on no man's
business ; laugh when I am merry, and claw no man in 15
his humor.

CONRADE Yea, but you must not make the full show of
this till you may do it without controlment. You have of 18
late stood out against your brother, and he hath ta'en 19
you newly into his grace, where it is impossible you
should take true root but by the fair weather that you
make yourself. It is needful that you frame the season
for your own harvest.

JOHN I had rather be a canker in a hedge than a rose in his 24
grace, and it better fits my blood to be disdained of all 25
than to fashion a carriage to rob love from any. In this, 26
though I cannot be said to be a flattering honest man, it
must not be denied but I am a plain-dealing villain. I am
trusted with a muzzle and enfranchised with a clog ; 29
therefore I have decreed not to sing in my cage. If I had
my mouth, I would bite ; if I had my liberty, I would do
my liking. In the meantime let me be that I am, and seek
not to alter me.

CONRADE Can you make no use of your discontent ?

JOHN I make all use of it, for I use it only. Who comes
here ? What news, Borachio ?
    Enter Borachio.

BORACHIO I came yonder from a great supper. The
Prince your brother is royally entertained by Leonato,

---

10 *born under Saturn* saturnine, ill-disposed; *moral* philosophical 11
mortifying mischief deadly disease 13 *stomach* appetite 15 *claw* flatter
18 *controlment* restraint 19 *stood out* rebelled 24 *canker* wild dog-rose
(despised as a weed) 25 *blood* humor, temper 26 *fashion a carriage*
assume a manner; *rob love* gain love undeserved 29 *with a muzzle* but
muzzled (i.e. not fully trusted); *enfranchised with a clog* freed, but with a
ball and chain

and I can give you intelligence of an intended marriage.

JOHN Will it serve for any model to build mischief on?

41 What is he for a fool that betroths himself to unquietness?

42 BORACHIO Marry, it is your brother's right hand.

JOHN Who? the most exquisite Claudio?

BORACHIO Even he.

45 JOHN A proper squire! And who? and who? which way looks he?

BORACHIO Marry, one Hero, the daughter and heir of Leonato.

49 JOHN A very forward March-chick! How came you to this?

51 BORACHIO Being entertained for a perfumer, as I was
52 smoking a musty room, comes me the Prince and
53 Claudio, hand in hand in sad conference. I whipt me
54 behind the arras and there heard it agreed upon that the Prince should woo Hero for himself, and having obtained her, give her to Count Claudio.

JOHN Come, come, let us thither. This may prove food to my displeasure. That young start-up hath all the glory of my overthrow. If I can cross him any way, I bless my-
60 self every way. You are both sure, and will assist me?

CONRADE To the death, my lord.

JOHN Let us to the great supper. Their cheer is the greater
63 that I am subdued. Would the cook were o' my mind!
64 Shall we go prove what's to be done?

BORACHIO We'll wait upon your lordship.

Exit [with others].

*

---

41 *What is he for a fool* what fool is he   42 *Marry* why, to be sure (originally an oath by the Virgin Mary)   45 *proper squire* fine fellow (contemptuous)
49 *forward March-chick* precocious youngster   51 *entertained for* hired as
52 *smoking* sweetening the odor with the smoke of burning juniper   53 *sad* serious   54 *arras* tapestry wall-hanging   60 *sure* trustworthy   63 *o' my mind* i.e. disposed to poison them   64 *prove* try

Enter Leonato, his brother [Antonio], Hero his   II, i
daughter, and Beatrice his niece [, also Margaret and
Ursula].

LEONATO Was not Count John here at supper?

ANTONIO I saw him not.

BEATRICE How tartly that gentleman looks! I never can 3
see him but I am heart-burned an hour after.   4

HERO He is of a very melancholy disposition.

BEATRICE He were an excellent man that were made just 6
in the midway between him and Benedick. The one is
too like an image and says nothing, and the other too like 8
my lady's eldest son, evermore tattling.   9

LEONATO Then half Signior Benedick's tongue in Count
John's mouth, and half Count John's melancholy in
Signior Benedick's face –

BEATRICE With a good leg and a good foot, uncle, and
money enough in his purse, such a man would win any
woman in the world – if 'a could get her good will.

LEONATO By my troth, niece, thou wilt never get thee a
husband if thou be so shrewd of thy tongue.   17

ANTONIO In faith, she's too curst.   18

BEATRICE Too curst is more than curst. I shall lessen
God's sending that way, for it is said, 'God sends a curst 20
cow short horns,' but to a cow too curst he sends none.

LEONATO So, by being too curst, God will send you no
horns.

BEATRICE Just, if he send me no husband; for the which 24
blessing I am at him upon my knees every morning and
evening. Lord, I could not endure a husband with a
beard on his face. I had rather lie in the woollen!   27

LEONATO You may light on a husband that hath no beard. 28

BEATRICE What should I do with him? dress him in my

II, i The hall of Leonato's house 3 *tartly* sourly 4 *am heart-burned* have
indigestion 6 *He were* that man would be 8 *image* statue 9 *my lady's
eldest son* a spoiled child who talks too much 17 *shrewd* satirical 18 *curst*
shrewish, ill-tempered 20 *that way* in that respect 24 *Just* exactly 27 *in
the woollen* between blankets without sheets 28 *light on* find

apparel and make him my waiting gentlewoman? He
that hath a beard is more than a youth, and he that hath
no beard is less than a man; and he that is more than a
youth is not for me; and he that is less than a man, I am
34 not for him. Therefore I will even take sixpence in
35 earnest of the berrord and lead his apes into hell.

LEONATO Well then, go you into hell?

BEATRICE No; but to the gate, and there will the devil
meet me like an old cuckold with horns on his head, and
say, 'Get you to heaven, Beatrice, get you to heaven.
Here's no place for you maids.' So deliver I up my apes,
41 and away to Saint Peter. For the heavens, he shows me
42 where the bachelors sit, and there live we as merry as the
day is long.

ANTONIO [to Hero] Well, niece, I trust you will be ruled
by your father.

45 BEATRICE Yes, faith. It is my cousin's duty to make cursy
and say, 'Father, as it please you.' But yet for all that,
cousin, let him be a handsome fellow, or else make another cursy, and say, 'Father, as it please me.'

LEONATO Well, niece, I hope to see you one day fitted
with a husband.

51 BEATRICE Not till God make men of some other metal
than earth. Would it not grieve a woman to be over-
mastered with a piece of valiant dust? to make an
54 account of her life to a clod of wayward marl? No, uncle,
I'll none. Adam's sons are my brethren, and truly I hold
56 it a sin to match in my kindred.

LEONATO Daughter, remember what I told you. If the
58 Prince do solicit you in that kind, you know your
answer.

BEATRICE The fault will be in the music, cousin, if you be

34-35 *in earnest* as deposit   35 *berrord* bear-ward (who often also kept
trained apes); *lead his apes* (the proverbial punishment of women who
die virgins)   41 *For the heavens* bound for heaven   42 *bachelors* unmarried
men and women   45 *make cursy* curtsy, show respect   51 *metal* material
54 *marl* clay, earth   56 *match . . . kindred* i.e. wed a brother   58 *solicit
. . . kind* propose

not wooed in good time. If the Prince be too important, 61
tell him there is measure in everything, and so dance out 62
the answer. For, hear me, Hero : wooing, wedding, and
repenting is as a Scotch jig, a measure, and a cinque- 64
pace : the first suit is hot and hasty like a Scotch jig (and
full as fantastical) ; the wedding, mannerly modest, as a
measure, full of state and ancientry ; and then comes 67
Repentance and with his bad legs falls into the cinque-
pace faster and faster, till he sink into his grave.

LEONATO Cousin, you apprehend passing shrewdly.   70
BEATRICE I have a good eye, uncle ; I can see a church by
daylight.
LEONATO The revellers are entering, brother. Make
good room.

> *Enter [masked] Prince [Don] Pedro, Claudio, and*
> *Benedick, and Balthasar ; [also, unmasked,]*
> *Don John [and Borachio, and musicians].*

PEDRO Lady, will you walk about with your friend ?   75
HERO So you walk softly and look sweetly and say noth-
ing, I am yours for the walk ; and especially when I walk
away.
PEDRO With me in your company ?
HERO I may say so when I please.
PEDRO And when please you to say so ?
HERO When I like your favor, for God defend the lute   82
should be like the case !
PEDRO My visor is Philemon's roof ; within the house is 84
Jove.
HERO Why then, your visor should be thatched.   86
PEDRO Speak low if you speak love.

> *[They step aside.]*

---

61 *important* importunate   62 *measure* moderation (but also a kind of
dance)   64 *cinque-pace* lively dance   67 *state* dignity ; *ancientry* traditional
formality   70 *apprehend passing shrewdly* perceive with unusual sharpness
75 *friend* a lover of either sex   82 *favor* face ; *defend* forbid, prevent   82–83
lute . . . case i.e. your face should be like your mask   84 *visor* mask ; *Philemon*
a peasant who entertained love and Mercury in his humble cottage   86
thatched i.e. whiskered

BALTHASAR Well, I would you did like me.

MARGARET So would not I for your own sake, for I have
90   many ill qualities.

BALTHASAR Which is one?

MARGARET I say my prayers aloud.

BALTHASAR I love you the better. The hearers may cry
amen.

MARGARET God match me with a good dancer!

BALTHASAR Amen.

MARGARET And God keep him out of my sight when the
97   dance is done! Answer, clerk.

BALTHASAR No more words. The clerk is answered.
      [They step aside.]

URSULA I know you well enough. You are Signior Antonio.

ANTONIO At a word, I am not.

101   URSULA I know you by the waggling of your head.

ANTONIO To tell you true, I counterfeit him.

103   URSULA You could never do him so ill-well unless you
104   were the very man. Here's his dry hand up and down.
      You are he, you are he!

ANTONIO At a word, I am not.

URSULA Come, come, do you think I do not know you by
your excellent wit? Can virtue hide itself? Go to, mum,
109   you are he. Graces will appear, and there's an end.
      [They step aside.]

BEATRICE Will you not tell me who told you so?

BENEDICK No, you shall pardon me.

BEATRICE Nor will you not tell me who you are?

BENEDICK Not now.

BEATRICE That I was disdainful, and that I had my good
115   wit out of the 'Hundred Merry Tales.' Well, this was
      Signior Benedick that said so.

---

90 *qualities* traits of character   97 *clerk* (the parish clerk read the respon-
ses in church services)   101 *waggling* palsied motion   103 *do him so ill-well*
imitate his ills so well   104 *dry hand* (a sign of age); *up and down* entirely
109 *Graces* good qualities   115 *Hundred Merry Tales* a popular jestbook

BENEDICK What's he?

BEATRICE I am sure you know him well enough.

BENEDICK Not I, believe me.

BEATRICE Did he never make you laugh?

BENEDICK I pray you, what is he?

BEATRICE Why, he is the Prince's jester, a very dull fool.
Only his gift is in devising impossible slanders. None but 123
libertines delight in him; and the commendation is not 124
in his wit, but in his villainy; for he both pleases men
and angers them, and then they laugh at him and beat
him. I am sure he is in the fleet. I would he had boarded 127
me.

BENEDICK When I know the gentleman, I'll tell him
what you say.

BEATRICE Do, do. He'll but break a comparison or two on 131
me; which peradventure, not marked or not laughed
at, strikes him into melancholy; and then there's a
partridge wing saved, for the fool will eat no supper 134
that night. [Music.] We must follow the leaders.

BENEDICK In every good thing.

BEATRICE Nay, if they lead to any ill, I will leave them at
the next turning.

Dance. Exeunt [all but Don John,
Borachio, and Claudio].

JOHN Sure my brother is amorous on Hero and hath
withdrawn her father to break with him about it. The
ladies follow her and but one visor remains.

BORACHIO And that is Claudio. I know him by his
bearing.

JOHN Are not you Signior Benedick?

CLAUDIO You know me well. I am he.

JOHN Signior, you are very near my brother in his love.
He is enamored on Hero. I pray you dissuade him from

---

123 *Only his gift* his only gift; *impossible* incredible   124 *libertines* free
thinkers, loose livers   127 *fleet* company of maskers (with play on sea-
fleet); *boarded* closed in on (nautical term)   131 *break a comparison* tilt
with words   134 *partridge wing* (considered a great delicacy)

47

her ; she is no equal for his birth. You may do the part of
an honest man in it.

CLAUDIO How know you he loves her ?

JOHN I heard him swear his affection.

BORACHIO So did I too, and he swore he would marry
her to-night.

153 JOHN Come, let us to the banquet.

Exeunt. Manet Claudio.

CLAUDIO

Thus answer I in name of Benedick
But hear these ill news with the ears of Claudio.
'Tis certain so. The Prince woos for himself.
Friendship is constant in all other things

158   Save in the office and affairs of love.
Therefore all hearts in love use their own tongues ;
Let every eye negotiate for itself
And trust no agent ; for beauty is a witch

162   Against whose charms faith melteth into blood.

163   This is an accident of hourly proof,

164   Which I mistrusted not. Farewell therefore Hero !

Enter Benedick.

BENEDICK Count Claudio ?

CLAUDIO Yea, the same.

BENEDICK Come, will you go with me ?

CLAUDIO Whither ?

BENEDICK Even to the next willow, about your own busi-

170   ness, County. What fashion will you wear the garland

171   of ? about your neck, like an usurer's chain ? or under
your arm, like a lieutenant's scarf ? You must wear it
one way, for the Prince hath got your Hero.

CLAUDIO I wish him joy of her.

---

153 *banquet* light repast of wine and sweets   158 *office* business, employment   162 *faith melteth* (as a witch melts the wax image of someone she
wishes to destroy); *blood* passion   163 *accident . . . proof* common occur-
rence   164 *mistrusted* suspected   170 *County* count; *garland* i.e. of willow,
symbol of forsaken love   171 *about your neck* i.e. as a symbol of wealth
171–72 *under your arm* i.e. gaily, as a symbol of honor

BENEDICK Why, that's spoken like an honest drovier. So 175
they sell bullocks. But did you think the Prince would
have served you thus?

CLAUDIO I pray you leave me.

BENEDICK Ho! now you strike like the blind man!'Twas 179
the boy that stole your meat, and you'll beat the post.

CLAUDIO If it will not be, I'll leave you.   *Exit.* 181

BENEDICK Alas, poor hurt fowl! now will he creep into
sedges. But, that my Lady Beatrice should know me, 183
and not know me! The Prince's fool! Ha! it may be I go
under that title because I am merry. Yea, but so I am
apt to do myself wrong. I am not so reputed. It is
the base (though bitter) disposition of Beatrice that 187
puts the world into her person and so gives me out. 188
Well, I'll be revenged as I may.

    Enter the Prince [Don Pedro], Hero, Leonato.

PEDRO Now, signior, where's the Count? Did you see
him?

BENEDICK Troth, my lord, I have played the part of Lady 191
Fame. I found him here as melancholy as a lodge in a 192
warren. I told him, and I think I told him true, that your
grace had got the good will of this young lady, and I
offered him my company to a willow tree, either to make
him a garland, as being forsaken, or to bind him up a
rod, as being worthy to be whipt.

PEDRO To be whipt? What's his fault?

BENEDICK The flat transgression of a schoolboy who, 199
being overjoyed with finding a bird's nest, shows it his
companion, and he steals it.

PEDRO Wilt thou make a trust a transgression? The transgression is in the stealer.

BENEDICK Yet it had not been amiss the rod had been

175 *drovier* drover, cattle trader   179 *the blind man* (unidentified allusion
to a proverb or familiar story)   181 *If . . . be* if you will not go   183 *sedges*
reeds   187 *bitter* biting   188 *puts . . . person* attributes to the world her own
personal feelings; *gives me out* reports me   191–92 *Lady Fame* bearer of
tidings   192–93 *lodge . . . warren* hutch in a rabbit warren (symbol of
melancholy)   199 *flat* plain

made, and the garland too; for the garland he might
have worn himself, and the rod he might have bestowed
on you, who, as I take it, have stolen his bird's nest.

PEDRO I will but teach them to sing and restore them to
the owner.

210 BENEDICK If their singing answer your saying, by my
faith you say honestly.

PEDRO The Lady Beatrice hath a quarrel to you. The
gentleman that danced with her told her she is much
213 wronged by you.

BENEDICK O, she misused me past the endurance of a
block! An oak but with one green leaf on it would have
answered her; my very visor began to assume life and
scold with her. She told me, not thinking I had been myself, that I was the Prince's jester, that I was duller than
220 a great thaw; huddling jest upon jest with such impos-
221 sible conveyance upon me that I stood like a man at a
mark, with a whole army shooting at me. She speaks
poniards, and every word stabs. If her breath were as
224 terrible as her terminations, there were no living near
225 her; she would infect to the North Star. I would not
marry her though she were endowed with all that Adam
had left him before he transgressed. She would have
228 made Hercules have turned spit, yea, and have cleft his
club to make the fire too. Come, talk not of her. You
230 shall find her the infernal Ate in good apparel. I would
231 to God some scholar would conjure her, for certainly,
while she is here, a man may live as quiet in hell as in a
sanctuary; and people sin upon purpose, because they

---

210 *If . . . saying* if it turns out as you say   213 *wronged* slandered   220
thaw (when roads are impassable and one must stay at home)   220–21
impossible conveyance incredible dexterity   221–22 *at a mark* beside a
target   224 *terminations* terms, i.e. name-calling   225 *infect* emit foul
odors (supposed to carry infection)   228 *Hercules . . . spit* (The Amazon
Omphale enslaved Hercules and set him to spinning. Turning a spit was an
even more humble chore, assigned to a boy or even a dog.)   230 *Ate* goddess of discord   231 *conjure her* (scholars were supposed to have the power
to call up or dismiss evil spirits)

would go thither; so indeed all disquiet, horror, and perturbation follows her.

Enter Claudio and Beatrice.

PEDRO Look, here she comes.

BENEDICK Will your grace command me any service to the world's end? I will go on the slightest errand now to the Antipodes that you can devise to send me on; I will fetch you a toothpicker now from the furthest inch of 239 Asia; bring you the length of Prester John's foot; fetch 240 you a hair off the great Cham's beard; do you any em- 241 bassage to the Pygmies – rather than hold three words' conference with this harpy. You have no employment 243 for me?

PEDRO None, but to desire your good company.

BENEDICK O God, sir, here's a dish I love not! I cannot endure my Lady Tongue.   *Exit.*

PEDRO Come, lady, come; you have lost the heart of Signior Benedick.

BEATRICE Indeed, my lord, he lent it me awhile, and I gave him use for it – a double heart for his single one. 250 Marry, once before he won it of me with false dice; therefore your grace may well say I have lost it.

PEDRO You have put him down, lady; you have put him down.

BEATRICE So I would not he should do me, my lord, lest I should prove the mother of fools. I have brought Count Claudio, whom you sent me to seek.

PEDRO Why, how now, Count? Wherefore are you sad?

CLAUDIO Not sad, my lord.

PEDRO How then? sick?

CLAUDIO Neither, my lord.

BEATRICE The Count is neither sad, nor sick, nor merry,

239 *toothpicker* toothpick 240 *Prester John* a fabulous monarch of the Far East 241 *Cham* Khan of Tartary, ruler of the Mongols 243 *harpy* a bird-woman, predatory and befouling 250 *use* interest, usury 250–52 *double heart ... lost it* (an obscure allusion; 'double' often meant deceitful, and this may be a taunt that Benedick can only get his heart away from her by trickery)

263 nor well ; but civil Count – civil as an orange, and some-
264 thing of that jealous complexion.

265 PEDRO I' faith, lady, I think your blazon to be true ;
266 though I'll be sworn, if he be so, his conceit is false.
Here, Claudio, I have wooed in thy name, and fair Hero
is won. I have broke with her father, and his good will
obtained. Name the day of marriage, and God give thee
joy !

LEONATO Count, take of me my daughter, and with her
271 my fortunes. His grace hath made the match, and all
grace say amen to it !

BEATRICE Speak, Count, 'tis your cue.

CLAUDIO Silence is the perfectest herald of joy. I were
but little happy if I could say how much. Lady, as you
are mine, I am yours. I give away myself for you and
dote upon the exchange.

BEATRICE Speak, cousin; or, if you cannot, stop his
mouth with a kiss and let not him speak neither.

PEDRO In faith, lady, you have a merry heart.

281 BEATRICE Yea, my lord ; I thank it, poor fool, it keeps on
282 the windy side of care. My cousin tells him in his ear
that he is in her heart.

CLAUDIO And so she doth, cousin.

285 BEATRICE Good Lord, for alliance ! Thus goes every one
286 to the world but I, and I am sunburnt. I may sit in a
287 corner and cry 'Heigh-ho for a husband !'

288 PEDRO Lady Beatrice, I will get you one.

289 BEATRICE I would rather have one of your father's getting.

---

263 *civil* grave, sober (with a pun on oranges of Seville)   264 *of . . . complexion* i.e. yellow (symbolic of jealousy)   265 *blazon* description (heraldic
term)   266 *conceit* conception, idea (with the additional suggestion here,
after *blazon*, of the fanciful device painted on a knight's shield)   271–72
all grace i.e. the Source of all grace   281 *fool* innocent creature   282 *windy*
windward, safe   285 *for alliance* (Claudio has just called her *cousin* in
anticipation of becoming her cousin by marriage)   285–86 *goes . . . world*
everybody gets married   286 *sunburnt* i.e. no longer fair   287 *Heigh-ho for
a husband* (from an old song)   288 *get* procure   289 *getting* begetting

Hath your grace ne'er a brother like you? Your father
got excellent husbands, if a maid could come by them.

PEDRO Will you have me, lady?

BEATRICE No, my lord, unless I might have another for
working days: your grace is too costly to wear every day.
But I beseech your grace pardon me. I was born to
speak all mirth and no matter.   296

PEDRO Your silence most offends me, and to be merry
best becomes you, for out o' question you were born in a
merry hour.

BEATRICE No, sure, my lord, my mother cried; but then
there was a star danced, and under that was I born.
Cousins, God give you joy!

LEONATO Niece, will you look to those things I told you
of?

BEATRICE I cry you mercy, uncle. By your grace's par-   304
don.   *Exit Beatrice.*

PEDRO By my troth, a pleasant-spirited lady.

LEONATO There's little of the melancholy element in her,
my lord. She is never sad but when she sleeps, and not
ever sad then; for I have heard my daughter say she
hath often dreamt of unhappiness and waked herself
with laughing.

PEDRO She cannot endure to hear tell of a husband.

LEONATO O, by no means! She mocks all her wooers out   311
of suit.

PEDRO She were an excellent wife for Benedick.

LEONATO O Lord, my lord! if they were but a week
married, they would talk themselves mad.

PEDRO County Claudio, when mean you to go to church?

CLAUDIO To-morrow, my lord. Time goes on crutches
till Love have all his rites.

---

296 *matter* substance   304 *cry you mercy* beg your pardon (for not having
done his bidding already)   304–05 *By your grace's pardon* excuse me
(addressed to the Prince)   311–12 *mocks . . . suit* makes fun of them until
they do not dare to woo her

LEONATO Not till Monday, my dear son, which is hence
a just sevennight; and a time too brief too, to have all
321 things answer my mind.

PEDRO Come, you shake the head at so long a breathing;
but I warrant thee, Claudio, the time shall not go dully
by us. I will in the interim undertake one of Hercules'
labors, which is, to bring Signior Benedick and the Lady
Beatrice into a mountain of affection th' one with th'
327 other. I would fain have it a match, and I doubt not but
to fashion it if you three will but minister such assist-
ance as I shall give you direction.

LEONATO My lord, I am for you, though it cost me ten
nights' watchings.

CLAUDIO And I, my lord.

PEDRO And you too, gentle Hero?

HERO I will do any modest office, my lord, to help my
cousin to a good husband.

PEDRO And Benedick is not the unhopefullest husband
that I know. Thus far can I praise him: he is of a noble
337 strain, of approved valor, and confirmed honesty. I will
teach you how to humor your cousin, that she shall fall
in love with Benedick; and I, *[to Leonato and Claudio]*
341 with your two helps, will so practice on Benedick that, in
342 despite of his quick wit and his queasy stomach, he shall
fall in love with Beatrice. If we can do this, Cupid is no
longer an archer; his glory shall be ours, for we are the
only love-gods. Go in with me, and I will tell you my
345 drift.   *Exit [with the others].*

*

II, ii   *Enter [Don] John and Borachio.*

JOHN It is so. The Count Claudio shall marry the daughter
of Leonato.

BORACHIO Yea, my lord; but I can cross it.

---

321 *answer my mind* as I wish them   327 *fain* gladly   337 *strain* family
341-42 *in despite* in spite   342 *queasy* delicate   345 *drift* plan
II, ii The house of Leonato

JOHN Any bar, any cross, any impediment will be medi- 4
cinable to me. I am sick in displeasure to him, and what- 5
soever comes athwart his affection ranges evenly with
mine. How canst thou cross this marriage?

BORACHIO Not honestly, my lord, but so covertly that no 8
dishonesty shall appear in me.

JOHN Show me briefly how.

BORACHIO I think I told your lordship, a year since, how
much I am in the favor of Margaret, the waiting gentlewoman to Hero.

JOHN I remember.

BORACHIO I can, at any unseasonable instant of the night,
appoint her to look out at her lady's chamber window.

JOHN What life is in that to be the death of this marriage?

BORACHIO The poison of that lies in you to temper. Go 18
you to the Prince your brother; spare not to tell him
that he hath wronged his honor in marrying the re-
nowned Claudio (whose estimation do you mightily 21
hold up) to a contaminated stale, such a one as Hero. 22

JOHN What proof shall I make of that?

BORACHIO Proof enough to misuse the Prince, to vex
Claudio, to undo Hero, and kill Leonato. Look you for
any other issue?

JOHN Only to despite them I will endeavor anything. 27

BORACHIO Go then; find me a meet hour to draw Don 28
Pedro and the Count Claudio alone; tell them that you
know that Hero loves me; intend a kind of zeal both to 30
the Prince and Claudio, as – in love of your brother's
honor, who hath made this match, and his friend's reputation, who is thus like to be cozened with the semblance 33
of a maid – that you have discovered thus. They will
scarcely believe this without trial. Offer them instances; 35

4 *medicinable* curative   5–7 *whatsoever . . . mine* whatever vexes him soothes
me   8 *covertly* secretly   18 *temper* compound, mix   21 *estimation*
reputation   22 *stale* prostitute   27 *despite* spite   28 *meet hour* suitable
time   30 *intend* pretend   33 *cozened* deceived, cheated; *semblance* outward
appearance   35 *instances* proofs

55

which shall bear no less likelihood than to see me at her chamber window, hear me call Margaret Hero, hear Margaret term me Claudio; and bring them to see this the very night before the intended wedding (for in the meantime I will so fashion the matter that Hero shall be absent) and there shall appear such seeming truth of

42 Hero's disloyalty that jealousy shall be called assurance and all the preparation overthrown.

JOHN Grow this to what adverse issue it can, I will put it in practice. Be cunning in the working this, and thy fee

46 is a thousand ducats.

BORACHIO Be you constant in the accusation, and my cunning shall not shame me.

49 JOHN I will presently go learn their day of marriage.

Exit [with Borachio].

*

II, iii   *Enter Benedick alone.*

BENEDICK Boy!

[*Enter Boy.*]

BOY Signior?

BENEDICK In my chamber window lies a book. Bring it hither to me in the orchard.

BOY I am here already, sir.

BENEDICK I know that, but I would have thee hence and here again. (*Exit [Boy].*) I do much wonder that one man, seeing how much another man is a fool when he dedicates his behaviors to love, will, after he hath laughed

10 at such shallow follies in others, become the argument of his own scorn by falling in love; and such a man is Claudio. I have known when there was no music with him but the drum and the fife; and now had he rather hear the tabor and the pipe. I have known when he would

15 have walked ten mile afoot to see a good armor; and now

---

42 *jealousy* suspicion; *assurance* proof   46 *ducats* gold coins   49 *presently* immediately

II, iii Leonato's orchard   10 *argument* subject   15 *armor* suit of armor

will he lie ten nights awake carving the fashion of a new　16
doublet. He was wont to speak plain and to the purpose,　17
like an honest man and a soldier; and now is he turned
orthography; his words are a very fantastical banquet –　19
just so many strange dishes. May I be so converted and　20
see with these eyes? I cannot tell; I think not. I will not be　21
sworn but love may transform me to an oyster; but I'll
take my oath on it, till he have made an oyster of me he
shall never make me such a fool. One woman is fair, yet
I am well; another is wise, yet I am well; another virtuous, yet I am well; but till all graces be in one woman,
one woman shall not come in my grace. Rich she shall
be, that's certain; wise, or I'll none; virtuous, or I'll
never cheapen her; fair, or I'll never look on her; mild,　29
or come not near me; noble, or not I for an angel; of　30
good discourse, an excellent musician, and her hair shall
be of what color it please God. Ha, the Prince and Mon-
sieur Love! [*retiring*] I will hide me in the arbor.　33

    Enter Prince [Don Pedro], Leonato, Claudio,
      Balthasar, with Music.

PEDRO
Come, shall we hear this music?

CLAUDIO
Yea, my good lord. How still the evening is,
As hushed on purpose to grace harmony!

PEDRO
See you where Benedick hath hid himself?

CLAUDIO
O, very well, my lord. The music ended,
We'll fit the kid-fox with a pennyworth.　39

PEDRO
Come, Balthasar, we'll hear that song again.

16 *carving* designing　**17** *doublet* jacket　**19** *orthography* pedantic in his choice and pronunciation of words　**20** *converted* changed　**21** *these eyes* the eyes of a lover　**29** *cheapen* bargain for　**30** *noble . . . angel* (play on the names of gold coins. The noble was worth about a third less than the angel.) **33** s.d. *Music* accompanists　**39** *fit . . . pennyworth* give the sly young fellow all he bargained for

BALTHASAR
O, good my lord, tax not so bad a voice
To slander music any more than once.

PEDRO
43   It is the witness still of excellency
44   To put a strange face on his own perfection.
I pray thee sing, and let me woo no more.

BALTHASAR
Because you talk of wooing, I will sing,
Since many a wooer doth commence his suit
To her he thinks not worthy, yet he woos,
Yet will he swear he loves.

PEDRO   Nay, pray thee come;
50   Or if thou wilt hold longer argument,
Do it in notes.

BALTHASAR   Note this before my notes:
There's not a note of mine that's worth the noting.

PEDRO
53   Why, these are very crotchets that he speaks!
54   Note notes, forsooth, and nothing!
[Music.]

BENEDICK [aside] Now divine air! Now is his soul
56   ravished! Is it not strange that sheep's guts should hale
souls out of men's bodies? Well, a horn for my money,
when all's done.
[Balthasar sings.]

The Song.

Sigh no more, ladies, sigh no more!
Men were deceivers ever,
One foot in sea, and one on shore;
To one thing constant never.

43 *witness* evidence   44 *put . . . on* pretend not to know   50 *argument*
talk   53 *crotchets* notes of half the value of a minim, very small notes
54 *nothing* (pronounced the same as *noting* above, and so punned on)
56 *hale* draw

Then sigh not so,
But let them go,
And be you blithe and bonny,
Converting all your sounds of woe
Into Hey nonny, nonny.

Sing no more ditties, sing no moe,
Of dumps so dull and heavy!   69
The fraud of men was ever so,
Since summer first was leavy.
Then sigh not so, &c.

PEDRO By my troth, a good song.

BALTHASAR And an ill singer, my lord.

PEDRO Ha, no, no, faith! Thou sing'st well enough for a
shift.   76

BENEDICK *[aside]* An he had been a dog that should have
howled thus, they would have hanged him; and I pray
God his bad voice bode no mischief. I had as live have   79
heard the night raven, come what plague could have   80
come after it.

PEDRO Yea, marry. Dost thou hear, Balthasar? I pray
thee get us some excellent music; for to-morrow night
we would have it at the Lady Hero's chamber window.

BALTHASAR The best I can, my lord.

PEDRO Do so. Farewell. *Exit Balthasar [with Musicians].*
Come hither, Leonato. What was it you told me of to-
day? that your niece Beatrice was in love with Signior
Benedick?

CLAUDIO O, ay! – *[aside to Pedro]* Stalk on, stalk on; the
fowl sits. – I did never think that lady would have loved
any man.

LEONATO No, nor I neither; but most wonderful that
she should so dote on Signior Benedick, whom she hath
in all outward behaviors seemed ever to abhor.

---

69 *dumps* sad songs, usually love songs   **76** *shift* emergency   **79** *live* lief,
willingly   **80** *night raven* (portent of disaster)

BENEDICK *[aside]* Is't possible? Sits the wind in that
corner?

LEONATO By my troth, my lord, I cannot tell what to
98 think of it, but that she loves him with an enraged
99 affection, it is past the infinite of thought.

PEDRO May be she doth but counterfeit.

CLAUDIO Faith, like enough.

LEONATO O God, counterfeit? There was never counterfeit of passion came so near the life of passion as she
104 discovers it.

PEDRO Why, what effects of passion shows she?

CLAUDIO *[aside]* Bait the hook well! This fish will bite.

LEONATO What effects, my lord? She will sit you – you
heard my daughter tell you how.

CLAUDIO She did indeed.

PEDRO How, how, I pray you? You amaze me. I would
have thought her spirit had been invincible against all
assaults of affection.

LEONATO I would have sworn it had, my lord – especially
against Benedick.

115 BENEDICK *[aside]* I should think this a gull but that the
white-bearded fellow speaks it. Knavery cannot, sure,
hide himself in such reverence.

118 CLAUDIO *[aside]* He hath ta'en th' infection. Hold it up.

PEDRO Hath she made her affection known to Benedick?

LEONATO No, and swears she never will. That's her torment.

CLAUDIO 'Tis true indeed. So your daughter says. 'Shall
I,' says she, 'that have so oft encountered him with
scorn, write to him that I love him?'

LEONATO This says she now when she is beginning to
write to him; for she'll be up twenty times a night, and
126 there will she sit in her smock till she have writ a sheet
of paper. My daughter tells us all.

---

98 *enraged* frenzied   **99** *infinite* furthest reach   **104** *discovers* reveals
115 *gull* hoax, trick   **118** *Hold* keep   **126** *smock* garment which served
both as slip and nightdress

CLAUDIO Now you talk of a sheet of paper, I remember a
pretty jest your daughter told us of.

LEONATO O, when she had writ it, and was reading it over,
she found 'Benedick' and 'Beatrice' between the sheet? 131

CLAUDIO That.

LEONATO O, she tore the letter into a thousand halfpence, 133
railed at herself that she should be so immodest to write
to one that she knew would flout her. 'I measure him,' 135
says she, 'by my own spirit; for I should flout him if he
writ to me. Yea, though I love him, I should.'

CLAUDIO Then down upon her knees she falls, weeps,
sobs, beats her heart, tears her hair, prays, curses – 'O
sweet Benedick! God give me patience!'

LEONATO She doth indeed; my daughter says so. And
the ecstasy hath so much overborne her that my 142
daughter is sometime afeard she will do a desperate out-
rage to herself. It is very true.

PEDRO It were good that Benedick knew of it by some
other, if she will not discover it.

CLAUDIO To what end? He would make but a sport of it
and torment the poor lady worse.

PEDRO An he should, it were an alms to hang him! She's 149
an excellent sweet lady, and (out of all suspicion) she is
virtuous.

CLAUDIO And she is exceeding wise.

PEDRO In everything but in loving Benedick.

LEONATO O, my lord, wisdom and blood combating in so 154
tender a body, we have ten proofs to one that blood hath
the victory. I am sorry for her, as I have just cause, being
her uncle and her guardian.

PEDRO I would she had bestowed this dotage on me. I 158
would have daffed all other respects and made her half 159

---

131 *between the sheet* in the folded sheet of paper, with pun on bedsheets
133 *halfpence* i.e. small pieces 135 *flout* mock 142 *ecstasy* excess of
passion 149 *an alms* a good deed 154 *blood* nature, natural feeling,
passion 158 *dotage* doting affection 159 *daffed* doffed, put aside;
respects considerations

myself. I pray you tell Benedick of it and hear what 'a will say.

LEONATO Were it good, think you?

CLAUDIO Hero thinks surely she will die; for she says she will die if he love her not, and she will die ere she make her love known, and she will die, if he woo her, rather
165 than she will bate one breath of her accustomed crossness.

166 PEDRO She doth well. If she should make tender of her love, 'tis very possible he'll scorn it; for the man (as you
168 know all) hath a contemptible spirit.

169 CLAUDIO He is a very proper man.

170 PEDRO He hath indeed a good outward happiness.

CLAUDIO Before God! and in my mind, very wise.

172 PEDRO He doth indeed show some sparks that are like wit.

CLAUDIO And I take him to be valiant.

PEDRO As Hector, I assure you; and in the managing of quarrels you may say he is wise, for either he avoids them with great discretion, or undertakes them with a most Christianlike fear.

LEONATO If he do fear God, 'a must necessarily keep peace. If he break the peace, he ought to enter into a quarrel with fear and trembling.

PEDRO And so will he do; for the man doth fear God,
182 howsoever it seems not in him by some large jests he will make. Well, I am sorry for your niece. Shall we go seek Benedick and tell him of her love?

CLAUDIO Never tell him, my lord. Let her wear it out
186 with good counsel.

LEONATO Nay, that's impossible; she may wear her heart out first.

PEDRO Well, we will hear further of it by your daughter. Let it cool the while. I love Benedick well, and I could

---

165 *bate* abate, give up   **166** *tender* offer   **168** *contemptible* contemptuous
169 *proper* handsome   **170** *outward happiness* attractive exterior   **172** *wit* intelligence   **182** *by* to judge by   **186** *counsel* reflection

wish he would modestly examine himself to see how
much he is unworthy so good a lady.

LEONATO My lord, will you walk? Dinner is ready.
[They walk away.]

CLAUDIO If he do not dote on her upon this, I will never
trust my expectation.

PEDRO Let there be the same net spread for her, and that
must your daughter and her gentlewomen carry. The   197
sport will be, when they hold one an opinion of another's 198
dotage, and no such matter. That's the scene that I
would see, which will be merely a dumb show. Let us   200
send her to call him in to dinner.
[Exeunt Don Pedro, Claudio, and Leonato.]

BENEDICK *[advancing]* This can be no trick. The conference was sadly borne; they have the truth of this from 203
Hero; they seem to pity the lady. It seems her affections 204
have their full bent. Love me? Why, it must be requited.
I hear how I am censured. They say I will bear myself
proudly if I perceive the love come from her. They say
too that she will rather die then give any sign of affection.
I did never think to marry. I must not seem proud.
Happy are they that hear their detractions and can put 210
them to mending. They say the lady is fair – 'tis a truth,
I can bear them witness; and virtuous – 'tis so, I cannot
reprove it; and wise, but for loving me – by my troth, it 213
is no addition to her wit, nor no great argument of her
folly, for I will be horribly in love with her. I may chance
have some odd quirks and remnants of wit broken on me 216
because I have railed so long against marriage. But doth
not the appetite alter? A man loves the meat in his youth
that he cannot endure in his age. Shall quips and senten- 219
ces and these paper bullets of the brain awe a man from 220

197 *carry* manage   198–99 *they . . . dotage* each thinks the other is in love
200 *dumb show* pantomime (because they can no longer carry on their usual
banter)   203 *sadly borne* seriously carried on   204–05 *affections . . . bent*
emotions are like a bow fully bent   210 *detractions* faults   213 *reprove*
disprove   216 *quirks* quips, quibbles   219 *sentences* maxims, wise sayings
220 *paper bullets* words; *awe* frighten

221 the career of his humor? No, the world must be peopled.
When I said I would die a bachelor, I did not think I
should live till I were married. Here comes Beatrice. By
this day, she's a fair lady! I do spy some marks of love
in her.

Enter Beatrice.

BEATRICE Against my will I am sent to bid you come in
to dinner.

BENEDICK Fair Beatrice, I thank you for your pains.

BEATRICE I took no more pains for those thanks than you
take pains to thank me. If it had been painful, I would
not have come.

BENEDICK You take pleasure then in the message?

BEATRICE Yea, just so much as you may take upon a
234 knive's point, and choke a daw withal. You have no
235 stomach, signior. Fare you well.   *Exit.*

BENEDICK Ha! 'Against my will I am sent to bid you
come in to dinner.' There's a double meaning in that. 'I
took no more pains for those thanks than you took pains
to thank me.' That's as much as to say, 'Any pains that I
take for you is as easy as thanks.' If I do not take pity of
her, I am a villain; if I do not love her, I am a Jew. I will
241 go get her picture.   *Exit.*

*

III, i   *Enter Hero and two Gentlewomen, Margaret and
Ursula.*

HERO
Good Margaret, run thee to the parlor.
There shalt thou find my cousin Beatrice
3 Proposing with the Prince and Claudio.
Whisper her ear and tell her, I and Ursley
Walk in the orchard, and our whole discourse

---

221 *career of his humor* action he fancies   234 *withal* with   235 *stomach*
appetite   241 *get her picture* i.e. so that he can 'feed his eyes' and so fall in
love
III, i Leonato's orchard   3 *Proposing* conversing

Is all of her. Say that thou overheard'st us;
And bid her steal into the pleachèd bower, 7
Where honeysuckles, ripened by the sun, 8
Forbid the sun to enter – like favorites,
Made proud by princes, that advance their pride
Against that power that bred it. There will she hide her
To listen our propose. This is thy office. 12
Bear thee well in it and leave us alone. 13

MARGARET

I'll make her come, I warrant you, presently.   *[Exit.]* 14

HERO

Now, Ursula, when Beatrice doth come,
As we do trace this alley up and down, 16
Our talk must only be of Benedick.
When I do name him, let it be thy part
To praise him more than ever man did merit.
My talk to thee must be how Benedick
Is sick in love with Beatrice. Of this matter
Is little Cupid's crafty arrow made,
That only wounds by hearsay.
          Enter Beatrice [and hides]. Now begin;
For look where Beatrice like a lapwing runs 24
Close by the ground, to hear our conference.

URSULA

The pleasant'st angling is to see the fish
Cut with her golden oars the silver stream 27
And greedily devour the treacherous bait.
So angle we for Beatrice, who even now
Is couchèd in the woodbine coverture. 30
Fear you not my part of the dialogue.

HERO

Then go we near her, that her ear lose nothing
Of the false sweet bait that we lay for it.

---

7 *pleachèd* hidden by thickly interwoven branches   **8** *ripened* brought to full
development   **12** *propose* conversation   **13** *leave us alone* leave the rest to us
14 *presently* immediately   **16** *trace* walk along   **24** *lapwing* kind of plover
27 *oars* i.e. fins   **30** *woodbine* i.e. honeysuckle

[They move.]
        No, truly, Ursula, she is too disdainful.
        I know her spirits are as coy and wild
36   As haggards of the rock.
    URSULA   But are you sure
        That Benedick loves Beatrice so entirely?
    HERO
        So says the Prince, and my new-trothèd lord.
    URSULA
        And did they bid you tell her of it, madam?
    HERO
        They did entreat me to acquaint her of it;
        But I persuaded them, if they loved Benedick,
        To wish him wrestle with affection
        And never to let Beatrice know of it.
    URSULA
        Why did you so? Doth not the gentleman
45   Deserve as full as fortunate a bed
        As ever Beatrice shall couch upon?
    HERO
        O god of love! I know he doth deserve
        As much as may be yielded to a man;
        But Nature never framed a woman's heart
        Of prouder stuff than that of Beatrice.
        Disdain and scorn ride sparkling in her eyes,
52   Misprizing what they look on; and her wit
        Values itself so highly that to her
        All matter else seems weak. She cannot love,
55   Nor take no shape nor project of affection,
        She is so self-endeared.
    URSULA   Sure I think so;
        And therefore certainly it were not good
        She knew his love, lest she'll make sport at it.
    HERO
        Why, you speak truth. I never yet saw man,

36 *haggards* hawks captured full grown and hard to tame   45 *as full* fully
52 *Misprizing* undervaluing, mistaking   55 *project* idea, notion

How wise, how noble, young, how rarely featured,
But she would spell him backward. If fair-faced,   61
She would swear the gentleman should be her sister;
If black, why, Nature, drawing of an antic,   63
Made a foul blot; if tall, a lance ill-headed;
If low, an agate very vilely cut;   65
If speaking, why, a vane blown with all winds;   66
If silent, why, a block movèd with none.
So turns she every man the wrong side out
And never gives to truth and virtue that
Which simpleness and merit purchaseth.   70

URSULA
Sure, sure, such carping is not commendable.   71

HERO
No, not to be so odd, and from all fashions,   72
As Beatrice is, cannot be commendable.
But who dare tell her so? If I should speak,
She would mock me into air; O, she would laugh me
Out of myself, press me to death with wit!   76
Therefore let Benedick, like covered fire,
Consume away in sighs, waste inwardly.
It were a better death than die with mocks,
Which is as bad as die with tickling.

URSULA
Yet tell her of it. Hear what she will say.

HERO
No; rather I will go to Benedick
And counsel him to fight against his passion.
And truly, I'll devise some honest slanders   84

---

61 *spell him backward* turn him inside out   63 *black* brunet; *antic* grotesque
figure, buffoon   65 *agate* figure carved on an agate and so very small   66
vane weathervane; *with* by   70 *simpleness* plain sincerity   71 *carping*
faultfinding   72 *from* contrary to   76 *press me to death* (the usual penalty
in England for refusing to plead guilty or not guilty. Weights were piled
on the victim's body until he either pleaded or died.)   84 *honest slanders*
adverse criticisms, but not of such a nature as to impugn her honesty
(i.e. her chastity)

To stain my cousin with. One doth not know
How much an ill word may empoison liking.

URSULA
O, do not do your cousin such a wrong!
She cannot be so much without true judgment
(Having so swift and excellent a wit
90   As she is prized to have) as to refuse
So rare a gentleman as Signior Benedick.

HERO
He is the only man of Italy,
Always excepted my dear Claudio.

URSULA
I pray you be not angry with me, madam,
Speaking my fancy: Signior Benedick,
96   For shape, for bearing, argument, and valor,
Goes foremost in report through Italy.

HERO
Indeed he hath an excellent good name.

URSULA
His excellence did earn it ere he had it.
When are you married, madam?

HERO
101   Why, every day to-morrow! Come, go in.
I'll show thee some attires, and have thy counsel
103   Which is the best to furnish me to-morrow.
        [They walk away.]

URSULA
104   She's limed, I warrant you! We have caught her, madam.

HERO
105   If it prove so, then loving goes by haps;
Some Cupid kills with arrows, some with traps.
                    [Exeunt Hero and Ursula.]

---

90 *prized* esteemed   **96** *bearing* deportment; *argument* discourse   **101**
every day to-morrow to-morrow and for ever after   **103** *furnish* dress
104 *limed* caught as with birdlime   **105** *haps* chance

BEATRICE *[coming forth from hiding]*
    What fire is in mine ears ? Can this be true ?   107
       Stand I condemned for pride and scorn so much ?
    Contempt, farewell ! and maiden pride, adieu !
       No glory lives behind the back of such.   110
    And, Benedick, love on ; I will requite thee,
       Taming my wild heart to thy loving hand.   112
    If thou dost love, my kindness shall incite thee
       To bind our loves up in a holy band ;
    For others say thou dost deserve, and I
    Believe it better than reportingly.   *Exit.* 116

*

    Enter Prince [Don Pedro], Claudio, Benedick, and   III, ii
    Leonato.

PEDRO I do but stay till your marriage be consummate,
    and then go I toward Arragon.
CLAUDIO I'll bring you thither, my lord, if you'll vouch- 3
    safe me.
PEDRO Nay, that would be as great a soil in the new gloss of
    your marriage as to show a child his new coat and forbid
    him to wear it. I will only be bold with Benedick for his 7
    company ; for, from the crown of his head to the sole of
    his foot, he is all mirth. He hath twice or thrice cut
    Cupid's bowstring, and the little hangman dare not shoot 10
    at him. He hath a heart as sound as a bell ; and his tongue
    is the clapper, for what his heart thinks, his tongue
    speaks.
BENEDICK Gallants, I am not as I have been.
LEONATO So say I Methinks you are sadder.   14

---

107 *What . . . ears* how my ears burn   110 *No . . . such* the proud and contemptuous are never praised except to their faces   112 *Taming . . . hand* (the
hawk figure again)   116 *better than reportingly* not merely as hearsay
III, ii The house of Leonato   3 *vouchsafe* permit   7 *be bold with* ask   10
hangman executioner, rogue   14 *sadder* more serious

CLAUDIO I hope he be in love.

16 PEDRO Hang him, truant! There's no true drop of blood
in him to be truly touched with love. If he be sad, he
wants money.

19 BENEDICK I have the toothache.

20 PEDRO Draw it.

BENEDICK Hang it!

CLAUDIO You must hang it first and draw it afterwards.

PEDRO What? sigh for the toothache?

24 LEONATO Where is but a humor or a worm.

25 BENEDICK Well, every one can master a grief but he that
has it.

CLAUDIO Yet say I he is in love.

28 PEDRO There is no appearance of fancy in him, unless it
29 be a fancy that he hath to strange disguises; as to be a
Dutchman to-day, a Frenchman to-morrow; or in the
shape of two countries at once, as a German from the
32 waist downward, all slops, and a Spaniard from the hip
upward, no doublet. Unless he have a fancy to this
34 foolery, as it appears he hath, he is no fool for fancy, as
you would have it appear he is.

CLAUDIO If he be not in love with some woman, there is
37 no believing old signs. 'A brushes his hat o' mornings.
What should that bode?

PEDRO Hath any man seen him at the barber's?

CLAUDIO No, but the barber's man hath been seen with
41 him, and the old ornament of his cheek hath already
stuffed tennis balls.

---

16 *truant* tramp (especially in love)   19 *toothache* (supposed to be common
among lovers)   20 *Draw* extract (but with punning reference below to
the hanging, drawing, and quartering of traitors)   24 *humor* one of the
four bodily fluids, in this case rheum; *worm* (supposed to cause toothache)
25 *grief* physical as well as mental pain   28–29 *fancy . . . fancy* love . . .
whim   29 *strange disguises* (the Englishman's dress was a perennial joke)
32 *slops* loose breeches   34 *fool for fancy* i.e. lover   37 *'A* he   41–42
ornament . . . balls i.e. his beard has been shaved (tennis balls were stuffed
with curled hair)

LEONATO Indeed he looks younger than he did, by the
loss of a beard.

PEDRO Nay, 'a rubs himself with civet. Can you smell 45
him out by that?

CLAUDIO That's as much as to say, the sweet youth's in
love.

PEDRO The greatest note of it is his melancholy.

CLAUDIO And when was he wont to wash his face?   49

PEDRO Yea, or to paint himself? for the which I hear
what they say of him.

CLAUDIO Nay, but his jesting spirit, which is now crept
into a lutestring, and now governed by stops.   53

PEDRO Indeed that tells a heavy tale for him. Conclude,
conclude, he is in love.

CLAUDIO Nay, but I know who loves him.

PEDRO That would I know too. I warrant, one that knows
him not.

CLAUDIO Yes, and his ill conditions; and in despite of all, 59
dies for him.

PEDRO She shall be buried with her face upwards.   61

BENEDICK Yet is this no charm for the toothache. Old 62
signior, walk aside with me. I have studied eight or nine
wise words to speak to you, which these hobby-horses   64
must not hear.   [Exeunt Benedick and Leonato.]

PEDRO For my life, to break with him about Beatrice!   66

CLAUDIO 'Tis even so. Hero and Margaret have by this
played their parts with Beatrice, and then the two bears
will not bite one another when they meet.

Enter John the Bastard.

JOHN My lord and brother, God save you

PEDRO Good den, brother.   71

---

45 _civet_ (a popular perfume) **49** _wash his face_ apply cosmetics **53** _stops_
fingerings, or positions marked for the fingers on the fingerboard of a lute,
the lover's instrument **59** _ill conditions_ bad qualities **61** _face upwards_
like a Christian (?), but probably with a ribald double intention **62** _charm_
i.e. cure; _Old_ (a term of respect) **64** _hobby-horses_ buffoons (originally
an antic figure in a morris dance) **66** _For my life_ upon my life **71** _Good
den_ good evening

JOHN If your leisure served, I would speak with you.

PEDRO In private?

JOHN If it please you. Yet Count Claudio may hear, for
what I would speak of concerns him.

PEDRO What's the matter?

JOHN [to Claudio] Means your lordship to be married to-
morrow?

PEDRO You know he does.

JOHN I know not that, when he knows what I know.

81 CLAUDIO If there be any impediment, I pray you discover
it.

JOHN You may think I love you not. Let that appear here-
83 after, and aim better at me by that I now will manifest.
84 For my brother, I think he holds you well and in dear-
85 ness of heart hath holp to effect your ensuing marriage –
surely suit ill spent and labor ill bestowed!

PEDRO Why, what's the matter?

88 JOHN I came hither to tell you, and, circumstances short-
89 ened (for she has been too long a-talking of), the lady is
90 disloyal.

CLAUDIO Who? Hero?

JOHN Even she – Leonato's Hero, your Hero, every
man's Hero.

CLAUDIO Disloyal?

95 JOHN The word is too good to paint out her wickedness. I
could say she were worse; think you of a worse title, and
97 I will fit her to it. Wonder not till further warrant. Go
but with me to-night, you shall see her chamber window
entered, even the night before her wedding day. If you
love her then, to-morrow wed her. But it would better
fit your honor to change your mind.

CLAUDIO May this be so?

PEDRO I will not think it.

---

81 *discover* disclose   83 *aim . . . me* judge better of me   84–85 *dearness of heart* friendship   85 *holp* helped   88–89 *circumstances shortened* circumstantial details omitted   89 *a-talking of* talked of   90 *disloyal* unfaithful   95 *paint out* portray   97 *till further warrant* till further assured by proof

JOHN If you dare not trust that you see, confess not that 104
you know. If you will follow me, I will show you enough;
and when you have seen more and heard more, proceed
accordingly.

CLAUDIO If I see anything to-night why I should not
marry her to-morrow, in the congregation where I 109
should wed there will I shame her.

PEDRO And, as I wooed for thee to obtain her, I will join
with thee to disgrace her.

JOHN I will disparage her no farther till you are my wit-
nesses. Bear it coldly but till midnight, and let the issue 114
show itself.

PEDRO O day untowardly turned! 116

CLAUDIO O mischief strangely thwarting!

JOHN O plague right well prevented! 118
So will you say when you have seen the sequel. *[Exeunt.]*

*

Enter Dogberry and his compartner [Verges], with III, iii
the Watch.

DOGBERRY Are you good men and true?

VERGES Yea, or else it were pity but they should suffer sal- 2
vation, body and soul.

DOGBERRY Nay, that were a punishment too good for
them if they should have any allegiance in them, being 5
chosen for the Prince's watch. 6

VERGES Well, give them their charge, neighbor Dogberry. 7

DOGBERRY First, who think you the most desartless man 8
to be constable? 9

1 . WATCH Hugh Oatcake, sir, or George Seacole, for
they can write and read.

104 *that* what 109 *congregation* company 114 *coldly* coolly 116
untowardly unfavorably, unluckily 118 *plague* misfortune; *prevented*
forestalled
III, iii A street in Messina 2 *salvation* (his mistake for 'damnation')
5 *allegiance* (for 'treachery') 6 *watch* men chosen to police the streets
at night 7 *charge* instructions 8 *desartless* (for 'deserving') 9 *constable*
deputy leader of the watch (Dogberry is the *right master constable*)

DOGBERRY Come hither, neighbor Seacole. God hath
13   blessed you with a good name. To be a well-favored man
is the gift of fortune, but to write and read comes by
nature.

2. WATCH Both which, master constable –

DOGBERRY You have. I knew it would be your answer.
17   Well, for your favor, sir, why, give God thanks and
make no boast of it; and for your writing and reading,
let that appear when there is no need of such vanity. You
20   are thought here to be the most senseless and fit man for
the constable of the watch. Therefore bear you the lant-
22   horn. This is your charge: you shall comprehend all
23   vagrom men; you are to bid any man stand, in the
Prince's name.

2. WATCH How if 'a will not stand?

DOGBERRY Why then, take no note of him, but let him
go, and presently call the rest of the watch together and
thank God you are rid of a knave.

VERGES If he will not stand when he is bidden, he is none
of the Prince's subjects.

DOGBERRY True, and they are to meddle with none but
the Prince's subjects. You shall also make no noise in the
streets; for, for the watch to babble and to talk is most
34   tolerable, and not to be endured.

1. WATCH We will rather sleep than talk. We know what
36   belongs to a watch.

37 DOGBERRY Why, you speak like an ancient and most
quiet watchman, for I cannot see how sleeping should
39   offend. Only have a care that your bills be not stolen.
Well, you are to call at all the alehouses and bid those
that are drunk get them to bed.

2. WATCH How if they will not?

---

13 *well-favored* handsome   17 *favor* appearance   20 *senseless* (for 'sensible')   22 *comprehend* (for 'apprehend')   23 *vagrom* vagrant   34 *tolerable* (for 'intolerable')   36 *belongs to* is the duty of   37 *ancient* elderly,
staid   39 *bills* halberds, long poles with combination axe and spear heads
carried chiefly as a badge of office

DOGBERRY Why then, let them alone till they are sober. If they make you not then the better answer, you may say they are not the men you took them for.

2. WATCH Well, sir.

DOGBERRY If you meet a thief, you may suspect him, by virtue of your office, to be no true man; and for such 48 kind of men, the less you meddle or make with them, 49 why, the more is for your honesty.

2. WATCH If we know him to be a thief, shall we not lay hands on him?

DOGBERRY Truly, by your office you may; but I think they that touch pitch will be defiled. The most peace- 53 able way for you, if you do take a thief, is to let him show himself what he is, and steal out of your company.

VERGES You have been always called a merciful man, partner.

DOGBERRY Truly, I would not hang a dog by my will, much more a man who hath any honesty in him.

VERGES If you hear a child cry in the night, you must call to the nurse and bid her still it.

2. WATCH How if the nurse be asleep and will not hear us?

DOGBERRY Why then, depart in peace and let the child wake her with crying; for the ewe that will not hear her lamb when it baes will never answer a calf when he 66 bleats.

VERGES 'Tis very true.

DOGBERRY This is the end of the charge: you, constable, are to present the Prince's own person. If you meet the 69 Prince in the night, you may stay him.

VERGES Nay, by'r lady, that I think 'a cannot. 71

DOGBERRY Five shillings to one on't with any man that

---

48 *true* honest   49 *meddle or make* associate   53 *they . . . defiled* (para-phrased from Ecclesiasticus xiii, 1)   66 *calf* (Dogberry's comparison has led him to call the watchman a calf, or dolt)   69 *present* represent   71 *by'r lady* by Our Lady (a mild oath)

73   knows the statutes, he may stay him! Marry, not without
       the Prince be willing; for indeed the watch ought to
75   offend no man, and it is an offense to stay a man against
       his will.

VERGES By'r lady, I think it be so.

78 DOGBERRY Ha, ah, ha! Well, masters, good night. An
       there be any matter of weight chances, call up me. Keep
       your fellows' counsels and your own, and good night.
       Come, neighbor.

2. WATCH Well, masters, we hear our charge. Let us go sit
       here upon the church bench till two, and then all to
       bed.

DOGBERRY One word more, honest neighbors. I pray you
       watch about Signior Leonato's door, for the wedding
86   being there to-morrow, there is a great coil to-night.
87   Adieu. Be vigitant, I beseech you.

                              Exeunt [Dogberry and Verges].
                Enter Borachio and Conrade.

BORACHIO What, Conrade!

2. WATCH *[aside]* Peace! stir not!

BORACHIO Conrade, I say!

CONRADE Here, man. I am at thy elbow.

92 BORACHIO Mass, and my elbow itched! I thought there
93   would a scab follow.

94 CONRADE I will owe thee an answer for that; and now
       forward with thy tale.

96 BORACHIO Stand thee close then under this penthouse,
97   for it drizzles rain, and I will, like a true drunkard, utter
       all to thee.

2. WATCH *[aside]* Some treason, masters. Yet stand close.

73 *statutes* acts of Parliament (but the principle actually belongs to common
law) 75 *offense* (in the legal sense) 78 *Ha, ah, ha* (a pompous clearing
of the throat) 86 *coil* confusion, bustle 87 *vigitant* (for 'vigilant') 92
Mass a mild interjection (originally, by the Mass) 93 *scab* i.e. an itching
scab, with play on slang term for a scurvy fellow 94 *owe thee an answer*
answer that later 96 *penthouse* open shed with a sloping roof 97 *true
drunkard* (the word '*borracho*' is Spanish for 'drunkard,' and there was a
proverb, 'The drunkard tells all')

BORACHIO Therefore know I have earned of Don John a
thousand ducats.

CONRADE Is it possible that any villainy should be so
dear?   102

BORACHIO Thou shouldst rather ask if it were possible
any villainy should be so rich; for when rich villains
have need of poor ones, poor ones may make what price
they will.

CONRADE I wonder at it.

BORACHIO That shows thou art unconfirmed. Thou 108
knowest that the fashion of a doublet, or a hat, or a
cloak, is nothing to a man.

CONRADE Yes, it is apparel.

BORACHIO I mean the fashion.

CONRADE Yes, the fashion is the fashion.

BORACHIO Tush! I may as well say the fool's the fool.
But seest thou not what a deformed thief this fashion is? 115

1. WATCH [aside] I know that Deformed. 'A has been a
vile thief this seven year; 'a goes up and down like a 117
gentleman. I remember his name.

BORACHIO Didst thou not hear somebody?

CONRADE No; 'twas the vane on the house.   120

BORACHIO Seest thou not, I say, what a deformed thief
this fashion is? how giddily 'a turns about all the hot-
bloods between fourteen and five-and-thirty? sometimes fashioning them like Pharaoh's soldiers in the
reechy painting, sometime like god Bel's priests in the 125
old church window, sometime like the shaven Hercules 126
in the smirched worm-eaten tapestry, where his codpiece 127
seems as massy as his club?

CONRADE All this I see; and I see that the fashion wears
out more apparel than the man. But art not thou thyself

---

102 *dear* expensive 108 *unconfirmed* inexperienced in villainy 115
deformed thief deforming rascal 117 *goes up and down* walks about 120
vane weathervane 125 *reechy* grimy, smoky; *Bel's priests* the priests of
Baal (in the Apocryphal book of the Bible, 'Bel and the Dragon') 126
shaven Hercules (probably a confusion with Samson) 127 *codpiece* front
part of breeches, often stuffed and ornamented

giddy with the fashion too, that thou hast shifted out of
thy tale into telling me of the fashion?

BORACHIO Not so neither. But know that I have to-night
wooed Margaret, the Lady Hero's gentlewoman, by the
name of Hero. She leans me out at her mistress' chamber
window, bids me a thousand times good night – I tell
this tale vilely; I should first tell thee how the Prince,

138   Claudio, and my master, planted and placed and possessed by my master Don John, saw afar off in the or-

140   chard this amiable encounter.

CONRADE And thought they Margaret was Hero?

BORACHIO Two of them did, the Prince and Claudio;
but the devil my master knew she was Margaret; and

144   partly by his oaths, which first possessed them, partly
by the dark night, which did deceive them, but chiefly
by my villainy, which did confirm any slander that Don
John had made, away went Claudio enraged; swore he
would meet her, as he was appointed, next morning at
the temple, and there, before the whole congregation,
shame her with what he saw o'ernight and send her
home again without a husband.

1. WATCH We charge you in the Prince's name stand!

2. WATCH Call up the right master constable. We have

154   here recovered the most dangerous piece of lechery that
ever was known in the commonwealth.

1. WATCH And one Deformed is one of them. I know

157   him; 'a wears a lock.

CONRADE Masters, masters –

2. WATCH You'll be made bring Deformed forth, I warrant you.

CONRADE Masters –

162 2. WATCH Never speak, we charge you. Let us obey you
to go with us.

---

138 *possessed* deluded   140 *amiable encounter* lovers' meeting   144 *possessed*
took possession of   154 *recovered* (for 'discovered'); *lechery* (for 'treachery')
157 *lock* lovelock, a wisp of hair worn beside the left ear, often down to the
shoulder   162 *Let us obey you* (for 'we command you')

BORACHIO We are like to prove a goodly commodity, 164
  being taken up of these men's bills.   165
CONRADE A commodity in question, I warrant you. 166
  Come, we'll obey you.   *Exeunt.*

                           *

        Enter Hero, and Margaret and Ursula.   III, iv
HERO Good Ursula, wake my cousin Beatrice and desire
  her to rise.
URSULA I will, lady.
HERO And bid her come hither.
URSULA Well.   *[Exit.]*
MARGARET Troth, I think your other rebato were better. 6
HERO No, pray thee, good Meg, I'll wear this.
MARGARET By my troth, 's not so good, and I warrant
  your cousin will say so.
HERO My cousin's a fool, and thou art another. I'll wear
  none but this.
MARGARET I like the new tire within excellently, if the 12
  hair were a thought browner; and your gown's a most
  rare fashion, i' faith. I saw the Duchess of Milan's gown
  that they praise so.
HERO O, that exceeds, they say.
MARGARET By my troth, 's but a nightgown in respect of 17
  yours – cloth a gold and cuts, and laced with silver, set 18
  with pearls, down sleeves, side-sleeves, and skirts, round 19
  underborne with a bluish tinsel. But for a fine, quaint, 20

---

164 *commodity* merchandise   165 *taken up* (1) arrested, (2) accepted from a
usurer; *bills* (1) halberds, (2) bills of goods   166 *in question* (1) subject to
examination, (2) of doubtful quality
III, iv The house of Leonato   6 *rebato* stiff, flaring collar or ruff, usually
of starched or wired lace   12 *tire* head-dress with elaborate ornaments
attached; *within* in the next room   17 *nightgown* dressing gown   18
cuts slashes or notches to show the underbody; *laced with silver* with
silver threads applied, usually in a diagonal pattern   19 *down sleeves*
long sleeves; *side-sleeves* second, purely ornamental, sleeves hanging
open from the armhole   19–20 *round underborne* held out, stiffened from
underneath   20 *quaint* elegant

graceful, and excellent fashion, yours is worth ten on't.

HERO God give me joy to wear it! for my heart is exceeding heavy.

MARGARET 'Twill be heavier soon by the weight of a man.

HERO Fie upon thee! art not ashamed?

MARGARET Of what, lady? of speaking honorably? Is not
27 marriage honorable in a beggar? Is not your lord honorable without marriage? I think you would have me say,
29 'saving your reverence, a husband.' An bad thinking do
30 not wrest true speaking, I'll offend nobody. Is there any
harm in 'the heavier for a husband'? None, I think, an
it be the right husband and the right wife. Otherwise
33 'tis light, and not heavy. Ask my Lady Beatrice else.
Here she comes.

     Enter Beatrice.

35 HERO Good morrow, coz.

BEATRICE Good morrow, sweet Hero.

HERO Why, how now? Do you speak in the sick tune?

BEATRICE I am out of all other tune, methinks.

39 MARGARET Clap's into 'Light a love.' That goes without
40 a burden. Do you sing it, and I'll dance it.

41 BEATRICE Ye light a love with your heels! then, if your
husband have stables enough, you'll see he shall lack no
43 barnes.

MARGARET O illegitimate construction! I scorn that with
my heels.

BEATRICE 'Tis almost five o'clock, cousin; 'tis time you
were ready. By my troth, I am exceeding ill. Hey-ho!

MARGARET For a hawk, a horse, or a husband?

49 BEATRICE For the letter that begins them all, H.

---

27 *in* even in   29 *saving your reverence* (conventional apology for mention-
ing a delicate subject)   30 *wrest* twist, misunderstand   33 *light* (pun on
'wanton'); *else* if it be otherwise   35 *coz* cousin   39 *Clap's into* let us
begin briskly; *Light a love* (an old tune)   40 *burden* refrain (with a punning
reference to *heavier for a husband*)   41 *light . . . heels* i.e. grow wanton
43 *barnes* children (with an obvious pun)   49 *H* (with a play on 'ache,'
then pronounced 'aitch')

MARGARET Well, an you be not turned Turk, there's no 50
more sailing by the star.   51

BEATRICE What means the fool, trow?   52

MARGARET Nothing I; but God send every one their
heart's desire!

HERO These gloves the Count sent me, they are an excellent perfume.   56

BEATRICE I am stuffed, cousin; I cannot smell.   57

MARGARET A maid, and stuffed! There's goodly catch- 58
ing of cold.

BEATRICE O, God help me! God help me! How long
have you professed apprehension?   61

MARGARET Ever since you left it. Doth not my wit become me rarely?

BEATRICE It is not seen enough. You should wear it in 64
your cap. By my troth, I am sick.

MARGARET Get you some of this distilled *carduus bene-* 66
dictus and lay it to your heart. It is the only thing for a
qualm.   68

HERO There thou prick'st her with a thistle.

BEATRICE *Benedictus?* why *benedictus?* You have some
moral in this *benedictus*.   71

MARGARET Moral? No, by my troth, I have no moral
meaning; I meant plain holy thistle. You may think per-
chance that I think you are in love. Nay, by'r lady, I am
not such a fool to think what I list; nor I list not to think 74
what I can; nor indeed I cannot think, if I would think
my heart out of thinking, that you are in love, or that
you will be in love, or that you can be in love. Yet Benedick was such another, and now is he become a man. He 78

---

50 *turned Turk* i.e. turned pagan, changed 51 *star* North Star 52 *trow*
I wonder 56 *perfume* (gloves were often perfumed) 57 *I am stuffed* i.e.
my nose is stopped with a cold 58 *stuffed* pregnant 61 *professed apprehension* pretended to wit 64–65 *in your cap* (like a feather, where it would
show) 66–67 *carduus benedictus* holy thistle, regarded as a universal
remedy, with pun on 'Benedick' 68 *qualm* sudden faintness or pain 71
moral figurative meaning 74 *list* like, please 78 *a man* i.e. a normal man

80 swore he would never marry, and yet now in despite of his heart he eats his meat without grudging; and how you may be converted I know not, but methinks you look with your eyes as other women do.

BEATRICE What pace is this that thy tongue keeps?

84 MARGARET Not a false gallop.

Enter Ursula.

URSULA Madam, withdraw. The Prince, the Count, Signior Benedick, Don John, and all the gallants of the town are come to fetch you to church.

HERO Help to dress me, good coz, good Meg, good Ursula. *[Exeunt.]*

*

III, v   *Enter Leonato and the Constable [Dogberry] and the Headborough [Verges].*

LEONATO What would you with me, honest neighbor?

2 DOGBERRY Marry, sir, I would have some confidence
3 with you that decerns you nearly.

LEONATO Brief, I pray you, for you see it is a busy time with me.

DOGBERRY Marry, this it is, sir.

VERGES Yes, in truth it is, sir.

LEONATO What is it, my good friends?

DOGBERRY Goodman Verges, sir, speaks a little off the
10 matter – as old man, sir, and his wits are not so blunt as,
11 God help, I would desire they were; but, in faith, honest as the skin between his brows.

VERGES Yes, I thank God I am as honest as any man living that is an old man and no honester than I.

15 DOGBERRY Comparisons are odorous. Palabras, neighbor Verges.

80 *eats . . . grudging* has a normal appetite   84 *false gallop* canter, but the emphasis is on 'false'
III, v The house of Leonato   s.d. *Headborough* petty or local constable
2 *confidence* (for 'conference')   3 *decerns* (for 'concerns')   10 *blunt* (for 'sharp')   11–12 *honest . . . brows* (proverbial)   15 *odorous* (for 'odious');
Palabras from Spanish '*pocas palabras*,' (few words)

LEONATO Neighbors, you are tedious.

DOGBERRY It pleases your worship to say so, but we are
the poor Duke's officers; but truly, for mine own part, if 19
I were as tedious as a king, I could find in my heart to
bestow it all of your worship.

LEONATO All thy tediousness on me, ah?

DOGBERRY Yea, an 'twere a thousand pound more than
'tis; for I hear as good exclamation on your worship as 24
of any man in the city, and though I be but a poor man, I
am glad to hear it.

VERGES And so am I.

LEONATO I would fain know what you have to say.

VERGES Marry, sir, our watch to-night, excepting your 29
worship's presence, ha' ta'en a couple of as arrant
knaves as any in Messina.

DOGBERRY A good old man, sir; he will be talking. As 32
they say, 'When the age is in, the wit is out.' God help
us! it is a world to see! Well said, i' faith, neighbor Verges. Well, God's a good man. An two men ride of a
horse, one must ride behind. An honest soul, i' faith, sir,
by my troth he is, as ever broke bread; but God is to be
worshipped; all men are not alike, alas, good neighbor!

LEONATO Indeed, neighbor, he comes too short of you.

DOGBERRY Gifts that God gives.

LEONATO I must leave you.

DOGBERRY One word, sir. Our watch, sir, have indeed
comprehended two aspicious persons, and we would 43
have them this morning examined before your worship.

LEONATO Take their examination yourself and bring it
me. I am now in great haste, as it may appear unto you.

DOGBERRY It shall be suffigance.   47

LEONATO Drink some wine ere you go. Fare you well.
        [Enter a Messenger.]

---

19 *poor Duke's* (for 'Duke's poor')   24 *exclamation* (for 'acclamation')
29 *excepting* (for 'respecting')   32 ff. *As they say*, etc. (what follows is a
string of 'old ends' or stock phrases)   43 *comprehended* (for 'apprehended');
aspicious (for 'suspicious')   47 *suffigance* (for 'sufficient')

MESSENGER My lord, they stay for you to give your
daughter to her husband.

LEONATO I'll wait upon them. I am ready.

[Exeunt Leonato and Messenger.]

52 DOGBERRY Go, good partner, go get you to Francis
Seacole. Bid him bring his pen and inkhorn to the jail.

54 We are now to examination these men.

VERGES And we must do it wisely.

DOGBERRY We will spare for no wit, I warrant you. Here's

57 that shall drive some of them to a non-come. Only get

58 the learned writer to set down our excommunication,
and meet me at the jail.   *[Exeunt.]*

*

IV, i   *Enter Prince [Don Pedro], [John the] Bastard,*
Leonato, Friar [Francis], Claudio, Benedick, Hero,
and Beatrice [and Attendants].

LEONATO Come, Friar Francis, be brief. Only to the

2 plain form of marriage, and you shall recount their particular duties afterwards.

FRIAR You come hither, my lord, to marry this lady?

CLAUDIO No.

LEONATO To be married to her. Friar, you come to
marry her.

FRIAR Lady, you come hither to be married to this
count?

HERO I do.

10 FRIAR If either of you know any inward impediment why
you should not be conjoined, I charge you on your souls
to utter it.

52–53 *Francis Seacole* the Sexton or Town Clerk of IV, ii, not the same as
the George Seacole, constable of the watch, in III, iii, who could read and
write **54** *examination* (for 'examine') **57** *non-come* (abbreviation of '*non
compos mentis*,' but he probably means 'nonplus') **58** *excommunication* (for
'examination')
IV, i Within a church in Messina **2** *plain form* simple prescribed formula
2–3 *particular duties* the usual preliminary sermon on the duties of husband
and wife **10** *inward impediment* secret, or mental reservation

CLAUDIO Know you any, Hero?

HERO None, my lord.

FRIAR Know you any, Count?

LEONATO I dare make his answer – none.

CLAUDIO O, what men dare do! what men may do! what
men daily do, not knowing what they do!

BENEDICK How now? interjections? Why then, some be 19
of laughing, as, ah, ha, he!

CLAUDIO
Stand thee by, friar. Father, by your leave, 21
Will you with free and unconstrainèd soul
Give me this maid your daughter?

LEONATO
As freely, son, as God did give her me.

CLAUDIO
And what have I to give you back whose worth
May counterpoise this rich and precious gift? 26

PEDRO
Nothing, unless you render her again.

CLAUDIO
Sweet Prince, you learn me noble thankfulness. 28
There, Leonato, take her back again.
Give not this rotten orange to your friend.
She's but the sign and semblance of her honor.
Behold how like a maid she blushes here!
O, what authority and show of truth 33
Can cunning sin cover itself withal! 34
Comes not that blood as modest evidence
To witness simple virtue? Would you not swear, 36
All you that see her, that she were a maid,
By these exterior shows? But she is none:
She knows the heat of a luxurious bed; 39

19–20 *some . . . ah, ha, he* (he is quoting Lily's *Latin Grammar*, a standard text-
book of the day, which says of interjections, 'Some are of Laughing: as, Ha,
ha, ha.') 21 *Stand thee by* stand aside; *by your leave* if I may call you so 26
counterpoise weigh as much as 28 *Sweet* dear; *learn* teach 33 *authority*
assurance 34 *withal* with 36 *witness* bear witness to 39 *luxurious* lustful

Her blush is guiltiness, not modesty.

LEONATO
What do you mean, my lord?

CLAUDIO   Not to be married,
42   Not to knit my soul to an approvèd wanton.

LEONATO
43   Dear my lord, if you, in your own proof,
      Have vanquished the resistance of her youth
      And made defeat of her virginity –

CLAUDIO
      I know what you would say. If I have known her,
      You will say she did embrace me as a husband,
48   And so extenuate the forehand sin.
      No, Leonato,
50   I never tempted her with word too large,
      But, as a brother to his sister, showed
      Bashful sincerity and comely love.

HERO
      And seemed I ever otherwise to you?

CLAUDIO
54   Out on thee seeming! I will write against it.
55   You seem to me as Dian in her orb,
56   As chaste as is the bud ere it be blown;
57   But you are more intemperate in your blood
      Than Venus, or those pamp'red animals
      That rage in savage sensuality.

HERO
60   Is my lord well that he doth speak so wide?

LEONATO
      Sweet Prince, why speak not you?

PEDRO   What should I speak?
62   I stand dishonored that have gone about

42 *approvèd* proved   43 *proof* experience   48 *extenuate . . . sin* excuse the
sin of anticipating the marriage state   50 *large* broad, immodest   54 *Out*
shame   55 *Dian* Diana, goddess of chastity; *orb* sphere, the moon   56
blown in blossom   57 *intemperate* ungoverned   60 *wide* far from the truth
62 *gone about* undertaken

To link my dear friend to a common stale.   63

LEONATO

Are these things spoken, or do I but dream?

JOHN

Sir, they are spoken, and these things are true.

BENEDICK

This looks not like a nuptial.

HERO   'True'! O God!

CLAUDIO

Leonato, stand I here?
Is this the Prince? Is this the Prince's brother?
Is this face Hero's? Are our eyes our own?

LEONATO

All this is so; but what of this, my lord?

CLAUDIO

Let me but move one question to your daughter,
And by that fatherly and kindly power   72
That you have in her, bid her answer truly.

LEONATO

I charge thee do so, as thou art my child.

HERO

O, God defend me! How am I beset!
What kind of catechising call you this?

CLAUDIO

To make you answer truly to your name.

HERO

Is it not Hero? Who can blot that name
With any just reproach?

CLAUDIO   Marry, that can Hero!
Hero itself can blot out Hero's virtue.   80
What man was he talked with you yesternight,
Out at your window betwixt twelve and one?
Now, if you are a maid, answer to this.   83

HERO

I talked with no man at that hour, my lord.

---

63 *stale* harlot   72 *kindly* natural   80 *Hero itself* i.e. the name by which he had heard Borachio call Margaret   83 *answer to* explain

PEDRO
Why, then are you no maiden. Leonato,
I am sorry you must hear. Upon mine honor
87   Myself, my brother, and this grievèd Count
Did see her, hear her, at that hour last night
Talk with a ruffian at her chamber window,
90   Who hath indeed, most like a liberal villain,
Confessed the vile encounters they have had
A thousand times in secret.

JOHN
Fie, fie! they are not to be named, my lord –
Not to be spoke of;
There is not chastity enough in language
Without offense to utter them. Thus, pretty lady,
97   I am sorry for thy much misgovernment.

CLAUDIO
O Hero! what a Hero hadst thou been
If half thy outward graces had been placed
About thy thoughts and counsels of thy heart!
But fare thee well, most foul, most fair! Farewell,
Thou pure impiety and impious purity!
For thee I'll lock up all the gates of love,
104   And on my eyelids shall conjecture hang,
To turn all beauty into thoughts of harm,
And never shall it more be gracious.

LEONATO
Hath no man's dagger here a point for me?
      [Hero swoons.]

BEATRICE
Why, how now, cousin? Wherefore sink you down?

JOHN
Come let us go. These things, come thus to light,
110   Smother her spirits up.
      [Exeunt Don Pedro, Don John, and Claudio.]

87 *grievèd* aggrieved, wronged   90 *liberal* libertine   97 *much misgovernment* great misconduct   104 *conjecture* doubt, suspicion   110 *spirits* vital
powers

BENEDICK
How doth the lady?
BEATRICE   Dead, I think. Help, uncle!
Hero! why, Hero! Uncle! Signior Benedick! Friar!
LEONATO
O Fate, take not away thy heavy hand!
Death is the fairest cover for her shame
That may be wished for.
BEATRICE   How now, cousin Hero?
FRIAR Have comfort, lady.
LEONATO Dost thou look up?   117
FRIAR Yea, wherefore should she not?
LEONATO
Wherefore? Why, doth not every earthly thing
Cry shame upon her? Could she here deny
The story that is printed in her blood?   120
Do not live, Hero; do not ope thine eyes;
For, did I think thou wouldst not quickly die,
Thought I thy spirits were stronger than thy shames,
Myself would on the rearward of reproaches   124
Strike at thy life. Grieved I, I had but one?
Chid I for that at frugal nature's frame?   126
O, one too much by thee! Why had I one?
Why ever wast thou lovely in my eyes?
Why had I not with charitable hand
Took up a beggar's issue at my gates,
Who smirchèd thus and mired with infamy,
I might have said, 'No part of it is mine;
This shame derives itself from unknown loins'?
But mine, and mine I loved, and mine I praised,
And mine that I was proud on – mine so much
That I myself was to myself not mine,   136
Valuing of her – why she, O, she is fall'n
Into a pit of ink, that the wide sea

117 *look up* (a sign of innocence)   120 *printed in her blood* written in her
blushes   124 *on . . . reproaches* after reproaching you   126 *frame* plan,
design   136 *I myself . . . mine* I lost or forgot myself

　　　　　Hath drops too few to wash her clean again,
140　　　And salt too little which may season give
　　　　　To her foul tainted flesh!

BENEDICK Sir, sir, be patient. For my part, I am so
attired in wonder, I know not what to say.

BEATRICE

O, on my soul, my cousin is belied!

BENEDICK

Lady, were you her bedfellow last night?

BEATRICE

No, truly, not; although, until last night,
I have this twelvemonth been her bedfellow.

LEONATO

Confirmed, confirmed! O, that is stronger made
Which was before barred up with ribs of iron!
Would the two princes lie? and Claudio lie,
Who loved her so that, speaking of her foulness,
Washed it with tears? Hence from her! let her die.

FRIAR

　　　　　Hear me a little;
　　　　　For I have only been silent so long,
155　　　And given way unto this course of fortune,
　　　　　By noting of the lady. I have marked
157　　　A thousand blushing apparitions
　　　　　To start into her face, a thousand innocent shames
　　　　　In angel whiteness beat away those blushes,
　　　　　And in her eye there hath appeared a fire
161　　　To burn the errors that these princes hold
　　　　　Against her maiden truth. Call me a fool;
　　　　　Trust not my reading nor my observations,
164　　　Which with experimental seal doth warrant
　　　　　The tenure of my book; trust not my age,
　　　　　My reverence, calling, nor divinity,

140 *season give* provide a preservative　155 *course of fortune* turn of events
157 *blushing apparitions* blushes (personified)　161 *errors* (personified as heretics)　164 *experimental seal* seal of experience　164–65 *warrant . . . book* confirm my interpretation of her expression (my book)

    If this sweet lady lie not guiltless here
    Under some biting error.

LEONATO   Friar, it cannot be.
    Thou seest that all the grace that she hath left
    Is that she will not add to her damnation
    A sin of perjury : she not denies it.
    Why seek'st thou then to cover with excuse
    That which appears in proper nakedness ?

FRIAR
    Lady, what man is he you are accused of ?

HERO
    They know that do accuse me ; I know none.
    If I know more of any man alive
    Than that which maiden modesty doth warrant,
    Let all my sins lack mercy ! O my father,
    Prove you that any man with me conversed
    At hours unmeet, or that I yesternight   180
    Maintained the change of words with any creature,   181
    Refuse me, hate me, torture me to death !   182

FRIAR
    There is some strange misprision in the princes.   183

BENEDICK
    Two of them have the very bent of honor ;   184
    And if their wisdoms be misled in this,
    The practice of it lives in John the bastard,   186
    Whose spirits toil in frame of villainies.   187

LEONATO
    I know not. If they speak but truth of her,
    These hands shall tear her. If they wrong her honor,
    The proudest of them shall well hear of it.
    Time hath not yet so dried this blood of mine,
    Nor age so eat up my invention,   192
    Nor fortune made such havoc of my means,

---

180 *unmeet* improper **181** *Maintained* carried on; *change* exchange
182 *Refuse* disown **183** *misprision* mistake **184** *bent* shape, form **186**
practice plotting **187** *in frame of* in framing **192** *invention* power to make
plans

Nor my bad life reft me so much of friends,
195 But they shall find awaked in such a kind
196 Both strength of limb and policy of mind,
Ability in means, and choice of friends,
198 To quit me of them throughly.

FRIAR   Pause awhile
And let my counsel sway you in this case.
200 Your daughter here the princess (left for dead),
201 Let her awhile be secretly kept in,
And publish it that she is dead indeed ;
203 Maintain a mourning ostentation,
And on your family's old monument
Hang mournful epitaphs, and do all rites
That appertain unto a burial.

LEONATO
What shall become of this ? What will this do ?

FRIAR
208 Marry, this well carried shall on her behalf
Change slander to remorse. That is some good.
But not for that dream I on this strange course,
211 But on this travail look for greater birth.
She dying, as it must be so maintained,
Upon the instant that she was accused,
Shall be lamented, pitied, and excused
Of every hearer ; for it so falls out
216 That what we have we prize not to the worth
Whiles we enjoy it, but being lacked and lost,
218 Why, then we rack the value, then we find
The virtue that possession would not show us
Whiles it was ours. So will it fare with Claudio.

---

195 *kind* manner   196 *policy of mind* mental power   198 *quit me of* settle
accounts with; *throughly* thoroughly   200 *princess* (so in quarto and folio
texts, although Hero is not, in this version of the story, a princess. Perhaps a
courtesy title, or perhaps an author's inconsistency.)   201 *in* at home
203 *mourning ostentation* formal show of mourning   208 *carried* managed
211 *on this travail* as a result of this effort   216 *to the worth* for what it is
worth   218 *rack* stretch as on a torture rack

When he shall hear she died upon his words,
Th' idea of her life shall sweetly creep   222
Into his study of imagination,   223
And every lovely organ of her life   224
Shall come apparelled in more precious habit,   225
More moving, delicate, and full of life,
Into the eye and prospect of his soul
Than when she lived indeed. Then shall he mourn
(If ever love had interest in his liver)   229
And wish he had not so accusèd her –
No, though he thought his accusation true.
Let this be so, and doubt not but success   232
Will fashion the event in better shape   233
Than I can lay it down in likelihood.
But if all aim but this be levelled false,   235
The supposition of the lady's death
Will quench the wonder of her infamy.
And if it sort not well, you may conceal her,   238
As best befits her wounded reputation,
In some reclusive and religious life,   240
Out of all eyes, tongues, minds, and injuries.

BENEDICK
Signior Leonato, let the friar advise you ;
And though you know my inwardness and love   243
Is very much unto the Prince and Claudio,
Yet, by mine honor, I will deal in this
As secretly and justly as your soul
Should with your body.

LEONATO   Being that I flow in grief,   247
The smallest twine may lead me.

---

222 *idea . . . life* i.e. memory of her   223 *his . . . imagination* the thoughts of
his musing hours   224 *organ of her life* part of her when she was alive   225
habit apparel   229 *liver* (the presumed physiological seat of love, in contrast
to the heart, the romantic seat)   232 *success* what succeeds or follows, i.e.
the course of time   233 *event* outcome   235 *be levelled false* be directed
falsely (and so miss the mark)   238 *sort* turn out   240 *reclusive* cloistered
243 *inwardness* intimacy   247 *flow* am afloat (and hence easily pulled)

FRIAR
    'Tis well consented. Presently away ;
250   For to strange sores strangely they strain the cure.
    Come, lady, die to live. This wedding day
252   Perhaps is but prolonged. Have patience and endure.
                    Exit [with all but Beatrice and Benedick].

BENEDICK Lady Beatrice, have you wept all this while ?

BEATRICE Yea, and I will weep a while longer.

BENEDICK I will not desire that.

BEATRICE You have no reason. I do it freely.

BENEDICK Surely I do believe your fair cousin is wronged.

BEATRICE Ah, how much might the man deserve of me
    that would right her !

BENEDICK Is there any way to show such friendship ?

261 BEATRICE A very even way, but no such friend.

BENEDICK May a man do it ?

BEATRICE It is a man's office, but not yours.

BENEDICK I do love nothing in the world so well as you.
    Is not that strange ?

BEATRICE As strange as the thing I know not. It were as
    possible for me to say I loved nothing so well as you.
    But believe me not ; and yet I lie not. I confess nothing,
    nor I deny nothing. I am sorry for my cousin.

BENEDICK By my sword, Beatrice, thou lovest me.

271 BEATRICE Do not swear and eat it.

BENEDICK I will swear by it that you love me, and I will
    make him eat it that says I love not you.

BEATRICE Will you not eat your word ?

BENEDICK With no sauce that can be devised to it. I
275   protest I love thee.

BEATRICE Why then, God forgive me !

BENEDICK What offense, sweet Beatrice ?

279 BEATRICE You have stayed me in a happy hour. I was
    about to protest I loved you.

---

250 *strain the cure* i.e. use desperate remedies **252** *prolonged* deferred
261 *even* direct **271** *swear and eat it* i.e. eat the words of this oath, go back
on it **275** *protest* solemnly affirm **279** *stayed* stopped

BENEDICK And do it with all thy heart.

BEATRICE I love you with so much of my heart that none
is left to protest.

BENEDICK Come, bid me do anything for thee.

BEATRICE Kill Claudio.

BENEDICK Ha! not for the wide world!

BEATRICE You kill me to deny it. Farewell.

BENEDICK Tarry, sweet Beatrice.

BEATRICE I am gone, though I am here. There is no love
in you. Nay, I pray you let me go.

BENEDICK Beatrice –

BEATRICE In faith, I will go.

BENEDICK We'll be friends first.

BEATRICE You dare easier be friends with me than fight
with mine enemy.

BENEDICK Is Claudio thine enemy?

BEATRICE Is 'a not approved in the height a villain, that 297
hath slandered, scorned, dishonored my kinswoman? O
that I were a man! What? bear her in hand until they 299
come to take hands, and then with public accusation, 300
uncovered slander, unmitigated rancor – O God, that I 301
were a man! I would eat his heart in the market place.

BENEDICK Hear me, Beatrice –

BEATRICE Talk with a man out at a window! – a proper
saying!

BENEDICK Nay, but Beatrice –

BEATRICE Sweet Hero! she is wronged, she is slandered,
she is undone. 308

BENEDICK Beat –

BEATRICE Princes and Counties! Surely a princely testi- 310
mony, a goodly count, Count Comfect, a sweet gallant 311
surely! O that I were a man for his sake! or that I had
any friend would be a man for my sake! But manhood is

---

297 *approved* proved; *height* highest degree **299** *bear her in hand* lead her
on, delude her **300** *take hands* marry **301** *uncovered* undisguised **308**
undone ruined **310** *Counties* counts **311** *count* legal indictment (with a
pun on Claudio's title); *Comfect* comfit, sugar-candy

314   melted into cursies, valor into compliment, and men are
only turned into tongue, and trim ones too. He is now as
valiant as Hercules that only tells a lie, and swears it. I
cannot be a man with wishing; therefore I will die a
woman with grieving.

BENEDICK Tarry, good Beatrice. By this hand, I love
thee.

BEATRICE Use it for my love some other way than swear-
ing by it.

BENEDICK Think you in your soul the Count Claudio
hath wronged Hero?

BEATRICE Yea, as sure as I have a thought or a soul.

BENEDICK Enough, I am engaged. I will challenge him.
I will kiss your hand, and so I leave you. By this hand,
Claudio shall render me a dear account. As you hear of
me, so think of me. Go comfort your cousin. I must say
she is dead – and so farewell.   *[Exeunt.]*

*

IV, ii   *Enter the Constables [Dogberry and Verges] and the
Town Clerk [Sexton] in gowns, Borachio [, Conrade,
and Watch].*

1 DOGBERRY Is our whole dissembly appeared?

VERGES O, a stool and a cushion for the sexton.

SEXTON Which be the malefactors?

DOGBERRY Marry, that am I and my partner.

5 VERGES Nay, that's certain. We have the exhibition to
examine.

SEXTON But which are the offenders that are to be examined? let them come before master constable.

DOGBERRY Yea, marry, let them come before me. What
is your name, friend?

BORACHIO Borachio.

---

314 *cursies* curtsies
IV, ii A hearing-room in Messina   1 *dissembly* (for 'assembly')   5 *exhibition* (for 'commission')

DOGBERRY Pray write down Borachio. Yours, sirrah? 12

CONRADE I am a gentleman, sir, and my name is Conrade.

DOGBERRY Write down Master Gentleman Conrade.
Masters, do you serve God?

BOTH Yea, sir, we hope.

DOGBERRY Write down that they hope they serve God;
and write God first, for God defend but God should go 18
before such villains! Masters, it is proved already that
you are little better than false knaves, and it will go near
to be thought so shortly. How answer you for yourselves?

CONRADE Marry, sir, we say we are none.

DOGBERRY A marvellous witty fellow, I assure you; but
I will go about with him. *[to Borachio]* Come you 24
hither, sirrah. A word in your ear. Sir, I say to you, it is
thought you are false knaves.

BORACHIO Sir, I say to you we are none.

DOGBERRY Well, stand aside. Fore God, they are both in 28
a tale. Have you writ down that they are none?

SEXTON Master constable, you go not the way to examine. You must call forth the watch that are their accusers.

DOGBERRY Yea, marry, that's the eftest way. Let the 32
watch come forth. Masters, I charge you in the Prince's
name accuse these men.

1. WATCH This man said, sir, that Don John the Prince's
brother was a villain.

DOGBERRY Write down Prince John a villain. Why, this
is flat perjury, to call a prince's brother villain.

BORACHIO Master constable –

DOGBERRY Pray thee, fellow, peace. I do not like thy 40
look, I promise thee.

SEXTON What heard you him say else?

2. WATCH Marry, that he had received a thousand ducats

12 *sirrah* sir (a derogatory form, resented by Conrade) 18 *defend* forbid
24 *go about with* undertake, deal with 28–29 *they . . . tale* both tell the same
story 32 *eftest* easiest, quickest

of Don John for accusing the Lady Hero wrongfully.

DOGBERRY Flat burglary as ever was committed.

VERGES Yea, by mass, that it is.

SEXTON What else, fellow?

1 . WATCH And that Count Claudio did mean, upon his words, to disgrace Hero before the whole assembly, and not marry her.

DOGBERRY O villain! thou wilt be condemned into ever-
52   lasting redemption for this.

SEXTON What else?

WATCHMEN This is all.

SEXTON And this is more, masters, than you can deny. Prince John is this morning secretly stolen away. Hero was in this manner accused, in this very manner refused, and upon the grief of this suddenly died. Master constable, let these men be bound and brought to Leonato's. I will go before and show him their examination. *[Exit.]*

61 DOGBERRY Come, let them be opinioned.

VERGES Let them be in the hands –

63 CONRADE Off, coxcomb!

DOGBERRY God's my life, where's the sexton? Let him write down the Prince's officer coxcomb. Come, bind
66   them. – Thou naughty varlet!

CONRADE Away! you are an ass, you are an ass.

68 DOGBERRY Dost thou not suspect my place? Dost thou not suspect my years? O that he were here to write me down an ass! But, masters, remember that I am an ass. Though it be not written down, yet forget not that I am
72   an ass. No, thou villain, thou art full of piety, as shall be proved upon thee by good witness. I am a wise fellow; and which is more, an officer; and which is more, a householder; and which is more, as pretty a piece of flesh as any is in Messina, and one that knows the law,

---

52 *redemption* (for 'damnation')   61 *opinioned* (for 'pinioned')   63 *coxcomb* fool (derived from the comb of red flannel worn on the head of a professional court jester)   66 *naughty* wicked; *varlet* scoundrel   68 *suspect* (for 'respect')   72 *piety* (for 'impiety')

go to ! and a rich fellow enough, go to ! and a fellow that
hath had losses ; and one that hath two gowns and every-   77
thing handsome about him. Bring him away. O that I
had been writ down an ass !   *Exit [with the others].*

*

Enter Leonato and his brother [Antonio].   V, i

ANTONIO
  If you go on thus, you will kill yourself,
  And 'tis not wisdom thus to second grief   2
  Against yourself.
LEONATO   I pray thee cease thy counsel,
  Which falls into mine ears as profitless
  As water in a sieve. Give not me counsel,
  Nor let no comforter delight mine ear
  But such a one whose wrongs do suit with mine.   7
  Bring me a father that so loved his child,
  Whose joy of her is overwhelmed like mine,   9
  And bid him speak of patience.
  Measure his woe the length and breadth of mine,
  And let it answer every strain for strain,   12
  As thus for thus, and such a grief for such,
  In every lineament, branch, shape, and form.
  If such a one will smile and stroke his beard,   15
  Bid sorrow wag, cry 'hem' when he should groan,   16
  Patch grief with proverbs, make misfortune drunk
  With candle-wasters – bring him yet to me,   18
  And I of him will gather patience.
  But there is no such man ; for, brother, men
  Can counsel and speak comfort to that grief
  Which they themselves not feel ; but, tasting it,
  Their counsel turns to passion, which before

___

77 *had losses* (implying that he had had possessions to lose)
V, i A street in Messina   2 *second* support, assist   7 *suit with* match
9 *overwhelmed* drowned, as with tears   12 *strain* trait   15 *stroke his
beard* (a gesture of complacency)   16 *wag* go away   18 *candle-wasters* i.e.
moral philosophers

24   Would give preceptial medicine to rage,
      Fetter strong madness in a silken thread,
26   Charm ache with air and agony with words.
      No, no ! 'Tis all men's office to speak patience
28   To those that wring under the load of sorrow,
      But no man's virtue nor sufficiency
      To be so moral when he shall endure
      The like himself. Therefore give me no counsel.
32   My griefs cry louder than advertisement.

ANTONIO
      Therein do men from children nothing differ.

LEONATO
      I pray thee peace. I will be flesh and blood ;
      For there was never yet philosopher
      That could endure the toothache patiently,
37   However they have writ the style of gods
38   And made a push at chance and sufferance.

ANTONIO
      Yet bend not all the harm upon yourself.
      Make those that do offend you suffer too.

LEONATO
      There thou speak'st reason. Nay, I will do so.
      My soul doth tell me Hero is belied ;
      And that shall Claudio know ; so shall the Prince,
      And all of them that thus dishonor her.
              Enter Prince [Don Pedro] and Claudio.

ANTONIO
      Here comes the Prince and Claudio hastily.

PEDRO
46   Good den, good den.

CLAUDIO   Good day to both of you.

LEONATO
      Hear you, my lords –

---

24 *preceptial medicine* remedy in the form of precepts   26 *Charm . . . air*
allay pain with talk   28 *wring* writhe   32 *advertisement* advice   37 *writ*
written in   38 *made a push* said pish, scoffed; *chance* mischance; *sufferance*
suffering   46 *Good den* good evening

PEDRO   We have some haste, Leonato.

LEONATO
    Some haste, my lord ! well, fare you well, my lord.
    Are you so hasty now ? Well, all is one.   49

PEDRO
    Nay, do not quarrel with us, good old man.

ANTONIO
    If he could right himself with quarrelling,
    Some of us would lie low.

CLAUDIO   Who wrongs him ?

LEONATO
    Marry, thou dost wrong me, thou dissembler, thou !   53
    Nay, never lay thy hand upon thy sword ;
    I fear thee not.

CLAUDIO   Marry, beshrew my hand   55
    If it should give your age such cause of fear.
    In faith, my hand meant nothing to my sword.

LEONATO
    Tush, tush, man ! never fleer and jest at me.   58
    I speak not like a dotard nor a fool,
    As under privilege of age to brag
    What I have done being young, or what would do,
    Were I not old. Know, Claudio, to thy head,
    Thou hast so wronged mine innocent child and me
    That I am forced to lay my reverence by   64
    And, with grey hairs and bruise of many days,   65
    Do challenge thee to trial of a man.   66
    I say thou hast belied mine innocent child.
    Thy slander hath gone through and through her heart,
    And she lies buried with her ancestors –
    O, in a tomb where never scandal slept,
    Save this of hers, framed by thy villainy !   71

---

49 *all is one* it does not matter   **53** *thou* (distinguished from the more respectful 'you' with which he addresses the Prince)   **55** *beshrew* (mild curse)   **58** *fleer* jeer   **64** *lay . . . by* renounce the respect due to old age **65** *bruise* wear and tear   **66** *trial of a man* manly trial, i.e. a duel   **71** *framed* made

CLAUDIO
My villainy?

LEONATO   Thine, Claudio; thine I say.

PEDRO
You say not right, old man.

LEONATO   My lord, my lord,
I'll prove it on his body if he dare,
75   Despite his nice fence and his active practice,
76   His May of youth and bloom of lustihood.

CLAUDIO
Away! I will not have to do with you.

LEONATO
78   Canst thou so daff me? Thou hast killed my child.
If thou kill'st me, boy, thou shalt kill a man.

ANTONIO
He shall kill two of us, and men indeed.
But that's no matter; let him kill one first.
82   Win me and wear me! Let him answer me.
Come, follow me, boy. Come, sir boy, come follow me.
84   Sir boy, I'll whip you from your foining fence!
Nay, as I am a gentleman, I will.

LEONATO
Brother –

ANTONIO
87   Content yourself. God knows I loved my niece,
And she is dead, slandered to death by villains,
That dare as well answer a man indeed
As I dare take a serpent by the tongue.
Boys, apes, braggarts, Jacks, milksops!

LEONATO   Brother Anthony –

ANTONIO
Hold you content. What, man! I know them, yea,
93   And what they weigh, even to the utmost scruple,

---

75 *nice fence* clever swordplay   76 *lustihood* vigor, strength   78 *daff* put
aside   82 *Win . . . wear me* (a proverb, serving as a form of challenge)
84 *foining* thrusting   87 *Content* calm   93 *scruple* smallest measure of
weight

Scambling, outfacing, fashion-monging boys,   94
That lie and cog and flout, deprave and slander,   95
Go anticly, show outward hideousness,   96
And speak off half a dozen dang'rous words,
How they might hurt their enemies, if they durst;
And this is all.

LEONATO
But, brother Anthony –

ANTONIO   Come, 'tis no matter.
Do not you meddle; let me deal in this.

PEDRO
Gentlemen both, we will not wake your patience.   102
My heart is sorry for your daughter's death;
But, on my honor, she was charged with nothing
But what was true, and very full of proof.   105

LEONATO
My lord, my lord –

PEDRO
I will not hear you.

LEONATO
No? Come, brother, away! – I will be heard.

ANTONIO
And shall, or some of us will smart for it.   *Exeunt ambo.*   109
        Enter Benedick.

PEDRO See, see! Here comes the man we went to seek.

CLAUDIO Now, signior, what news?

BENEDICK Good day, my lord.

PEDRO Welcome, signior. You are almost come to part   113
    almost a fray.

CLAUDIO We had liked to have had our two noses
    snapped off with two old men without teeth.

---

94 *Scambling* quarrelsome; *outfacing* impudent; *monging* mongering 95
cog cheat; *flout* jeer at; *deprave* defame 96 *anticly* fantastically dressed;
hideousness frightening aspect 102 *wake your patience* cause you to need
patience 105 *full of proof* fully proved 109 s.d. *ambo* both (Leonato and
Antonio) 113 *almost come* come almost in time

PEDRO Leonato and his brother. What think'st thou?
118   Had we fought, I doubt we should have been too young
for them.

BENEDICK In a false quarrel there is no true valor. I came
to seek you both.

CLAUDIO We have been up and down to seek thee; for
123   we are high-proof melancholy, and would fain have it
beaten away. Wilt thou use thy wit?

BENEDICK It is in my scabbard. Shall I draw it?

PEDRO Dost thou wear thy wit by thy side?

CLAUDIO Never any did so, though very many have been
128   beside their wit. I will bid thee draw, as we do the min-
strels – draw to pleasure us.

PEDRO As I am an honest man, he looks pale. Art thou
sick, or angry?

CLAUDIO What, courage, man! What though care killed
133   a cat, thou hast mettle enough in thee to kill care.

134 BENEDICK Sir, I shall meet your wit in the career an you
charge it against me. I pray you choose another subject.

CLAUDIO Nay then, give him another staff; this last was
137   broke cross.

PEDRO By this light, he changes more and more. I think
he be angry indeed.

140 CLAUDIO If he be, he knows how to turn his girdle.

BENEDICK Shall I speak a word in your ear?

CLAUDIO God bless me from a challenge!

BENEDICK [aside to Claudio] You are a villain. I jest not;
I will make it good how you dare, with what you dare,
145   and when you dare. Do me right, or I will protest your

---

118 *doubt* suspect   123 *high-proof* in a high degree of   128 *beside their wit*
out of their minds; *draw* (used of a sword, and of a minstrel's bow)   133
mettle vivacity   134 *in the career* while running at full speed   134–35
an you charge it if you charge with it (as with a lance in a tilt)   137 *broke
cross* broken across (as by an unskillful tilter)   140 *turn his girdle* prepare
for a bout, as in wrestling (?)   145 *Do me right* accept my challenge;
protest report abroad

cowardice. You have killed a sweet lady, and her death shall fall heavy on you. Let me hear from you.

CLAUDIO Well, I will meet you, so I may have good cheer.

PEDRO What, a feast? a feast?

CLAUDIO I' faith, I thank him, he hath bid me to a calve's   150
head and a capon, the which if I do not carve most curi-   151
ously, say my knife's naught. Shall I not find a wood-   152
cock too?

BENEDICK Sir, your wit ambles well; it goes easily.

PEDRO I'll tell thee how Beatrice praised thy wit the other   155
day. I said thou hadst a fine wit: 'True,' said she, 'a fine   156
little one.' 'No,' said I, 'a great wit.' 'Right,' says she, 'a
great gross one.' 'Nay,' said I, 'a good wit.' 'Just,' said
she, 'it hurts nobody.' 'Nay,' said I, 'the gentleman is
wise.' 'Certain,' said she, 'a wise gentleman,' 'Nay,' said   160
I, 'he hath the tongues.' 'That I believe,' said she, 'for he   161
swore a thing to me on Monday night which he forswore   162
on Tuesday morning. There's a double tongue; there's
two tongues.' Thus did she an hour together transshape   164
thy particular virtues. Yet at last she concluded with a
sigh, thou wast the properest man in Italy.   166

CLAUDIO For the which she wept heartily and said she
cared not.

PEDRO Yea, that she did; but yet, for all that, an if she did
not hate him deadly, she would love him dearly. The
old man's daughter told us all.

CLAUDIO All, all! and moreover, God saw him when he   172
was hid in the garden.

PEDRO But when shall we set the savage bull's horns on   174
the sensible Benedick's head?

---

150 *bid* invited; *calve's* calf's, i.e. fool's   **151** *capon* (another contemptuous allusion); *curiously* expertly   **152** *naught* good for nothing; *woodcock* bird famous for its stupidity   **155** *praised* appraised   **156** *fine* excellent, also small   **160** *wise gentleman* wiseacre   **161** *hath the tongues* can speak several languages   **162** *forswore* denied with an oath   **164** *transshape* transform   **166** *properest* handsomest   **172** *God saw him* (alluding to Genesis iii, 8, but also to the hoaxing of Benedick)   **174** *the savage bull's horns* (see I, i, 232 ff.)

176 CLAUDIO Yea, and text underneath, 'Here dwells Benedick, the married man'?

BENEDICK Fare you well, boy; you know my mind. I will
leave you now to your gossip-like humor. You break
jests as braggards do their blades, which God be thanked
hurt not. *[to the Prince]* My lord, for your many cour-
tesies I thank you. I must discontinue your company.
Your brother the bastard is fled from Messina. You have
among you killed a sweet and innocent lady. For my
Lord Lackbeard there, he and I shall meet; and till then
peace be with him.   *[Exit.]*

PEDRO He is in earnest.

CLAUDIO In most profound earnest; and, I'll warrant
you, for the love of Beatrice.

PEDRO And hath challenged thee?

CLAUDIO Most sincerely.

192 PEDRO What a pretty thing man is when he goes in his
doublet and hose and leaves off his wit!

*Enter Constables [Dogberry and Verges, with the
Watch, leading] Conrade and Borachio.*

194 CLAUDIO He is then a giant to an ape; but then is an ape a
doctor to such a man.

196 PEDRO But, soft you, let me be! Pluck up, my heart, and
be sad! Did he not say my brother was fled?

DOGBERRY Come you, sir. If justice cannot tame you, she
199 shall ne'er weigh more reasons in her balance. Nay, an
you be a cursing hypocrite once, you must be looked
to.

PEDRO How now? two of my brother's men bound?
Borachio one.

CLAUDIO Hearken after their offense, my lord.

PEDRO Officers, what offense have these men done?

---

176 *text* in capital letters   192–93 *in . . . hose* i.e. fully dressed   194–95 *a
giant . . . a man* much bigger than an ape, but the ape is much wiser than he
196–97 *Pluck . . . sad* pull up a moment, my mind, and be serious   199
balance scales (symbol of justice)

DOGBERRY Marry, sir, they have committed false report;
moreover, they have spoken untruths; secondarily, they
are slanders; sixth and lastly, they have belied a lady;
thirdly, they have verified unjust things; and to con-   208
clude, they are lying knaves.

PEDRO First, I ask thee what they have done; thirdly, I
ask thee what's their offense; sixth and lastly, why they
are committed; and to conclude, what you lay to their   212
charge.

CLAUDIO Rightly reasoned, and in his own division; and
by my troth there's one meaning well suited.   215

PEDRO Who have you offended, masters, that you are
thus bound to your answer? This learned constable is   217
too cunning to be understood. What's your offense?

BORACHIO Sweet Prince, let me go no farther to mine answer. Do you hear me, and let this Count kill me. I have
deceived even your very eyes. What your wisdoms could
not discover, these shallow fools have brought to light,
who in the night overheard me confessing to this man,
how Don John your brother incensed me to slander the   224
Lady Hero; how you were brought into the orchard and
saw me court Margaret in Hero's garments; how you
disgraced her when you should marry her. My villainy
they have upon record, which I had rather seal with my
death than repeat over to my shame. The lady is dead
upon mine and my master's false accusation; and briefly,
I desire nothing but the reward of a villain.

PEDRO Runs not this speech like iron through your   232
blood?

CLAUDIO I have drunk poison whiles he uttered it.

PEDRO But did my brother set thee on to this?

BORACHIO Yea, and paid me richly for the practice of it. 235

---

208 *verified* sworn to   **212** *committed* arrested and held for trial   **215** *well
suited* provided with several different suits, or modes of speech   **217** *bound
to your answer* bound over, indicted   **224** *incensed* incited   **232** *iron* a
sword   **235** *practice* accomplishment

PEDRO
> He is composed and framed of treachery,
> And fled he is upon this villainy.

CLAUDIO
> Sweet Hero, now thy image doth appear
> In the rare semblance that I loved it first.

240 DOGBERRY Come, bring away the plaintiffs. By this time
241 our sexton hath reformed Signior Leonato of the matter.
And, masters, do not forget to specify, when time and
place shall serve, that I am an ass.

VERGES Here, here comes Master Signior Leonato, and
the sexton too.

> *Enter Leonato, his brother [Antonio], and the Sexton.*

LEONATO
> Which is the villain? Let me see his eyes,
> That, when I note another man like him,
> I may avoid him. Which of these is he?

BORACHIO
> If you would know your wronger, look on me.

LEONATO
> Art thou the slave that with thy breath hast killed
> Mine innocent child?

BORACHIO   Yea, even I alone.

LEONATO
> No, not so, villain! thou beliest thyself.
> Here stand a pair of honorable men –
> A third is fled – that had a hand in it.
> I thank you princes for my daughter's death.
> Record it with your high and worthy deeds.

257 'Twas bravely done, if you bethink you of it.

CLAUDIO
258 I know not how to pray your patience;
> Yet I must speak. Choose your revenge yourself;
260 Impose me to what penance your invention

---

240 *plaintiffs* (for 'defendants') **241** *reformed* (for 'informed') **257** *bethink
you of* recall **258** *pray your patience* ask your forgiveness **260** *Impose me to*
impose on me

Can lay upon my sin. Yet sinned I not
But in mistaking.

PEDRO   By my soul, nor I!
And yet, to satisfy this good old man,
I would bend under any heavy weight
That he'll enjoin me to.

LEONATO
I cannot bid you bid my daughter live –
That were impossible; but I pray you both,
Possess the people in Messina here   268
How innocent she died; and if your love
Can labor aught in sad invention,
Hang her an epitaph upon her tomb,
And sing it to her bones – sing it to-night.
To-morrow morning come you to my house,
And since you could not be my son-in-law,
Be yet my nephew. My brother hath a daughter,
Almost the copy of my child that's dead,
And she alone is heir to both of us.
Give her the right you should have giv'n her cousin,   278
And so dies my revenge.

CLAUDIO   O noble sir!
Your over-kindness doth wring tears from me.
I do embrace your offer; and dispose   281
For henceforth of poor Claudio.

LEONATO
To-morrow then I will expect your coming;
To-night I take my leave. This naughty man
Shall face to face be brought to Margaret,
Who I believe was packed in all this wrong,   286
Hired to it by your brother.

BORACHIO   No, by my soul, she was not;
Nor knew not what she did when she spoke to me;

---

268 *Possess* inform   278 *right* right of becoming your wife (perhaps with
pun on 'rite' of marriage)   281 *dispose* you may dispose   286 *packed* in the
pact, an accomplice

But always hath been just and virtuous
In anything that I do know by her.

291 DOGBERRY Moreover, sir, which indeed is not under
white and black, this plaintiff here, the offender, did call
me ass. I beseech you let it be remembered in his punishment. And also the watch heard them talk of one De-
295 formed. They say he wears a key in his ear, and a lock
hanging by it, and borrows money in God's name, the
which he hath used so long and never paid that now
men grow hard-hearted and will lend nothing for God's
sake. Pray you examine him upon that point.

LEONATO I thank thee for thy care and honest pains.

DOGBERRY Your worship speaks like a most thankful
and reverent youth, and I praise God for you.

LEONATO There's for thy pains.
     [Gives money.]

304 DOGBERRY God save the foundation!

305 LEONATO Go, I discharge thee of thy prisoner, and I
thank thee.

DOGBERRY I leave an arrant knave with your worship,
which I beseech your worship to correct yourself, for
the example of others. God keep your worship! I wish
your worship well. God restore you to health! I humbly
311 give you leave to depart; and if a merry meeting may be
312 wished, God prohibit it! Come, neighbor.
     [Exeunt Dogberry and Verges.]

LEONATO
Until to-morrow morning, lords, farewell.

ANTONIO
Farewell, my lords. We look for you to-morrow.

PEDRO
We will not fail.

291–92 *under . . . black* in writing   **295** *key, lock* (his misunderstanding of
the *lock* of III, iii, 157)   **304** *God . . . foundation* (conventional phrase used
by beggars receiving alms at the gates of religious or charitable foundations)
305 *discharge* relieve   **311** *give you leave* (for 'ask your leave')   **312** *prohibit*
(for 'grant')

CLAUDIO   To-night I'll mourn with Hero.
                              [Exeunt Don Pedro and Claudio.]
LEONATO *[to the Watch]*
  Bring you these fellows on. – We'll talk with Margaret,
  How her acquaintance grew with this lewd fellow.   317
                              Exeunt.

*

     Enter Benedick and Margaret [meeting].   V, ii
BENEDICK Pray thee, sweet Mistress Margaret, deserve
  well at my hands by helping me to the speech of Beatrice.
MARGARET Will you then write me a sonnet in praise of
  my beauty?
BENEDICK In so high a style, Margaret, that no man 5
  living shall come over it; for in most comely truth thou
  deservest it.
MARGARET To have no man come over me? Why, shall I
  always keep below stairs?   9
BENEDICK. Thy wit is as quick as the greyhound's mouth
  – it catches.
MARGARET And yours 's as blunt as the fencer's foils,
  which hit but hurt not.
BENEDICK A most manly wit, Margaret: it will not hurt a
  woman. And so I pray thee call Beatrice. I give thee the
  bucklers.   16
MARGARET Give us the swords; we have bucklers of our
  own.
BENEDICK If you use them, Margaret, you must put in
  the pikes with a vice, and they are dangerous weapons 19
  for maids.
MARGARET Well, I will call Beatrice to you, who I think
  hath legs.   *Exit Margaret.*

317 *lewd* low, disreputable
V, ii Before Leonato's house 5 *style* i.e. of writing, but with a pun on
'stile,' a stairs over a fence 9 *keep below stairs* dwell in the servants'
quarters, i.e. never be mistress of a house 16 *bucklers* shields with spikes
in their centres (Margaret's retort is a ribald play on words) 19 *pikes*
spikes; *vice* screw

BENEDICK And therefore will come.

[Sings]   The god of love,
                  That sits above
               And knows me, and knows me,
               How pitiful I deserve –

28 I mean in singing; but in loving, Leander the good
29 swimmer, Troilus the first employer of panders, and a
30 whole book full of these quondam carpet-mongers,
    whose names yet run smoothly in the even road of a
32 blank verse – why, they were never so truly turned over
    and over as my poor self in love. Marry, I cannot show it
    in rhyme. I have tried. I can find out no rhyme to 'lady'
35 but 'baby' – an innocent rhyme; for 'scorn,' 'horn' – a
    hard rhyme; for 'school,' 'fool' – a babbling rhyme.
    Very ominous endings! No, I was not born under a
    rhyming planet, nor I cannot woo in festival terms.
         Enter Beatrice.
    Sweet Beatrice, wouldst thou come when I called thee?
BEATRICE Yea, signior, and depart when you bid me.
BENEDICK O, stay but till then!
BEATRICE 'Then' is spoken. Fare you well now. And yet,
    ere I go, let me go with that I came for, which is, with
    knowing what hath passed between you and Claudio.
BENEDICK Only foul words; and thereupon I will kiss
    thee.
BEATRICE Foul words is but foul wind, and foul wind is
47 but foul breath, and foul breath is noisome. Therefore I
    will depart unkissed.
BENEDICK Thou hast frighted the word out of his right
    sense, so forcible is thy wit. But I must tell thee plainly,
51 Claudio undergoes my challenge; and either I must

28 *Leander* (who swam the Hellespont every night to see another Hero
until he was drowned in a storm)   29 *Troilus* (who was helped to the love
of Cressida by her uncle Pandarus)   30 *quondam carpet-mongers* ancient
carpet knights (i.e. lovers rather than fighters)   32–33 *turned over and
over* head over heels   35 *innocent* childish   47 *noisome* offensive, bad-
smelling   51 *undergoes* bears

shortly hear from him or I will subscribe him a coward.   52
And I pray thee now tell me, for which of my bad parts
didst thou first fall in love with me?

BEATRICE For them all together, which maintained so
politic a state of evil that they will not admit any good   56
part to intermingle with them. But for which of my
good parts did you first suffer love for me?   58

BENEDICK Suffer love! – a good epithet. I do suffer love
indeed, for I love thee against my will.

BEATRICE In spite of your heart, I think. Alas, poor
heart! If you spite it for my sake, I will spite it for yours,
for I will never love that which my friend hates.

BENEDICK Thou and I are too wise to woo peaceably.

BEATRICE It appears not in this confession. There's not
one wise man among twenty that will praise himself.

BENEDICK An old, an old instance, Beatrice, that lived in
the time of good neighbors. If a man do not erect in this   68
age his own tomb ere he dies, he shall live no longer in
monument than the bell rings and the widow weeps.

BEATRICE And how long is that, think you?

BENEDICK Question: why, an hour in clamor and a quar-
ter in rheum. Therefore it is most expedient for the   73
wise, if Don Worm (his conscience) find no impediment
to the contrary, to be the trumpet of his own virtues, as I
am to myself. So much for praising myself, who, I
myself will bear witness, is praiseworthy. And now tell
me, how doth your cousin?

BEATRICE Very ill.

BENEDICK And how do you?

BEATRICE Very ill too.

BENEDICK Serve God, love me, and mend. There will I
leave you too, for here comes one in haste.

    Enter Ursula.

URSULA Madam, you must come to your uncle. Yonder's

52 *subscribe him* write him down   56 *politic* well organized   58 *suffer*
experience, but also feel the pain of   68 *time of good neighbors* i.e. Golden
age   73 *rheum* tears

113

85 old coil at home. It is proved my Lady Hero hath been
86 falsely accused, the Prince and Claudio mightily abused,
    and Don John is the author of all, who is fled and gone.
    Will you come presently?

BEATRICE Will you go hear this news, signior?

BENEDICK I will live in thy heart, die in thy lap, and be
    buried in thy eyes; and moreover, I will go with thee to
    thy uncle's.   *Exit [with Beatrice and Ursula].*

*

V, iii   *Enter Claudio, Prince [Don Pedro, Lord], and three
                or four with tapers [followed by Musicians].*

CLAUDIO Is this the monument of Leonato?
LORD It is, my lord.
CLAUDIO *[reads from a scroll]*

                        Epitaph.

              Done to death by slanderous tongues
4   Was the Hero that here lies.
5   Death, in guerdon of her wrongs,
                  Gives her fame which never dies.
              So the life that died with shame
              Lives in death with glorious fame.

        [Hangs up the scroll.]
              Hang thou there upon the tomb,
              Praising her when I am dumb.
    Now, music, sound, and sing your solemn hymn.

                  Song [by one attending].

12   Pardon, goddess of the night,
13   Those that slew thy virgin knight;

85 *old coil* confusion   86 *abused* deceived
V, iii A churchyard   4 *Hero* (pun intended)   5 *guerdon* reward   12 *goddess of the night* Diana, patroness of chastity   13 *virgin knight* (still punning
on *Hero*)

> For the which, with songs of woe,
> Round about her tomb they go.
> Midnight, assist our moan,
> Help us to sigh and groan
>   Heavily, heavily.
> Graves, yawn and yield your dead,
> Till death be utterèd   20
>   Heavily, heavily.

CLAUDIO Now unto thy bones good night!
> Yearly will I do this rite.

PEDRO
> Good morrow, masters. Put your torches out.
>   The wolves have preyed, and look, the gentle day,
> Before the wheels of Phoebus, round about   26
>   Dapples the drowsy east with spots of grey.
> Thanks to you all, and leave us. Fare you well.

CLAUDIO
> Good morrow, masters. Each his several way.

PEDRO
> Come, let us hence and put on other weeds,   30
>   And then to Leonato's we will go.

CLAUDIO
> And Hymen now with luckier issue speeds   32
>   Than this for whom we rend'red up this woe. *Exeunt.*

*

> *Enter Leonato, Benedick, [Beatrice,] Margaret,*   V, iv
> *Ursula, Old Man [Antonio], Friar [Francis], Hero.*

FRIAR
> Did I not tell you she was innocent?

---

20 *utterèd* fully expressed   26 *Phoebus* god who drives the chariot of the sun
30 *weeds* clothes   32 *Hymen* god of marriage; *speeds* (perhaps for 'speed us')
V, iv The hall in Leonato's house

LEONATO

So are the Prince and Claudio, who accused her

3   Upon the error that you heard debated.

But Margaret was in some fault for this,

5   Although against her will, as it appears

6   In the true course of all the question.

ANTONIO

7   Well, I am glad that all things sort so well.

BENEDICK

8   And so am I, being else by faith enforced

To call young Claudio to a reckoning for it.

LEONATO

Well, daughter, and you gentlewomen all,

Withdraw into a chamber by yourselves,

And when I send for you, come hither masked.

The Prince and Claudio promised by this hour

To visit me. You know your office, brother :

You must be father to your brother's daughter,

And give her to young Claudio.   *Exeunt Ladies.*

ANTONIO

17   Which I will do with confirmed countenance.

BENEDICK

Friar, I must entreat your pains, I think.

FRIAR

To do what, signior ?

BENEDICK

To bind me, or undo me – one of them.

Signior Leonato, truth it is, good signior,

Your niece regards me with an eye of favor.

LEONATO

That eye my daughter lent her. 'Tis most true.

BENEDICK

And I do with an eye of love requite her.

---

3 *Upon* because of   5 *against her will* unintentionally   6 *question* investigation   7 *sort* turn out   8 *faith* fidelity to my word   17 *confirmed countenance* straight face

LEONATO

 The sight whereof I think you had from me,
 From Claudio, and the Prince ; but what's your will ?

BENEDICK

 Your answer, sir, is enigmatical ;
 But, for my will, my will is, your good will
 May stand with ours, this day to be conjoined
 In the state of honorable marriage ;
 In which, good friar, I shall desire your help.

LEONATO

 My heart is with your liking.

FRIAR   And my help.
 Here comes the Prince and Claudio.

  Enter Prince [Don Pedro] and Claudio and two or
  three other.

PEDRO

 Good morrow to this fair assembly.

LEONATO

 Good morrow, Prince ; good morrow, Claudio.
 We here attend you. Are you yet determined   36
 To-day to marry with my brother's daughter ?

CLAUDIO

 I'll hold my mind, were she an Ethiope.   38

LEONATO

 Call her forth, brother. Here's the friar ready.

           [Exit Antonio.]

PEDRO

 Good morrow, Benedick. Why, what's the matter
 That you have such a February face,
 So full of frost, of storm, and cloudiness ?

CLAUDIO

 I think he thinks upon the savage bull.
 Tush, fear not, man ! We'll tip thy horns with gold,
 And all Europa shall rejoice at thee,   45

---

36 *yet* still   38 *Ethiope* i.e. black, and hence ugly in an age which admired
blondes   45 *Europa* Europe

117

46   As once Europa did at lusty Jove
      When he would play the noble beast in love.
BENEDICK
      Bull Jove, sir, had an amiable low,
      And some such strange bull leaped your father's cow
      And got a calf in that same noble feat
      Much like to you, for you have just his bleat.
            Enter [Leonato's] brother [Antonio], Hero, Beatrice,
            Margaret, Ursula [the ladies wearing masks].
CLAUDIO
52   For this I owe you. Here comes other reck'nings.
      Which is the lady I must seize upon?
ANTONIO
      This same is she, and I do give you her.
CLAUDIO
      Why then, she's mine. Sweet, let me see your face.
LEONATO
      No, that you shall not till you take her hand
      Before this friar and swear to marry her.
CLAUDIO
      Give me your hand before this holy friar.
      I am your husband if you like of me.
HERO
      And when I lived I was your other wife;
            [Unmasks.]
      And when you loved you were my other husband.
CLAUDIO
      Another Hero!
HERO   Nothing certainer.
63   One Hero died defiled; but I do live,
      And surely as I live, I am a maid.
PEDRO
      The former Hero! Hero that is dead!

46 *Europa* a girl who was wooed by Jove in the shape of a bull   52 *I owe you*
I will pay you later (Benedick has managed to call him both a calf and a
bastard); *reck'nings* bills to pay   63 *defiled* disgraced (by the false charge)

LEONATO
    She died, my lord, but whiles her slander lived.
FRIAR
    All this amazement can I qualify,   67
    When, after that the holy rites are ended,
    I'll tell you largely of fair Hero's death.   69
    Meantime let wonder seem familiar,   70
    And to the chapel let us presently.
BENEDICK
    Soft and fair, friar. Which is Beatrice ?
BEATRICE [unmasks]
    I answer to that name. What is your will ?
BENEDICK
    Do not you love me ?
BEATRICE   Why, no ; no more than reason.
BENEDICK
    Why, then your uncle, and the Prince, and Claudio
    Have been deceived – they swore you did.
BEATRICE
    Do not you love me ?
BENEDICK   Troth, no ; no more than reason.
BEATRICE
    Why, then my cousin, Margaret, and Ursula
    Are much deceived ; for they did swear you did.
BENEDICK
    They swore that you were almost sick for me.
BEATRICE
    They swore that you were well-nigh dead for me.
BENEDICK
    'Tis no such matter. Then you do not love me ?
BEATRICE
    No, truly, but in friendly recompense.   83

---

67 *qualify* moderate, relieve   69 *largely* in full   70 *let . . . familiar* treat this
marvel as if it were an ordinary matter   83 *friendly recompense* charitable
repayment

LEONATO
Come, cousin, I am sure you love the gentleman.

CLAUDIO
And I'll be sworn upon't that he loves her;
For here's a paper written in his hand,
A halting sonnet of his own pure brain,
Fashioned to Beatrice.

HERO   And here's another,
Writ in my cousin's hand, stol'n from her pocket,
Containing her affection unto Benedick.

91 BENEDICK A miracle! Here's our own hands against our
hearts. Come, I will have thee; but, by this light, I
take thee for pity.

BEATRICE I would not deny you; but, by this good day, I
yield upon great persuasion, and partly to save your life,
for I was told you were in a consumption.

BENEDICK Peace! I will stop your mouth.
          [Kisses her.]

PEDRO How dost thou, Benedick, the married man?

99 BENEDICK I'll tell thee what, Prince: a college of wit-
crackers cannot flout me out of my humor. Dost thou
think I care for a satire or an epigram? No. If a man will
102 be beaten with brains, 'a shall wear nothing handsome
about him. In brief, since I do purpose to marry, I will
think nothing to any purpose that the world can say
against it; and therefore never flout at me for what I
have said against it; for man is a giddy thing, and this is
my conclusion. For thy part, Claudio, I did think to
have beaten thee; but in that thou art like to be my
kinsman, live unbruised, and love my cousin.

CLAUDIO I had well hoped thou wouldst have denied
Beatrice, that I might have cudgelled thee out of thy

91 *hands* written testimony   99–100 *college of wit-crackers* assembly of
jokers   102 *beaten with brains* defeated with witticisms (but with a play on
the literal sense of having brains flung at him which will spoil his clothes)

single life, to make thee a double-dealer, which out of 112
question thou wilt be if my cousin do not look exceeding
narrowly to thee.

BENEDICK Come, come, we are friends. Let's have a
dance ere we are married, that we may lighten our own
hearts and our wives' heels.

LEONATO We'll have dancing afterward.

BENEDICK First, of my word! Therefore play, music. 119
Prince, thou art sad. Get thee a wife, get thee a wife!
There is no staff more reverent than one tipped with 121
horn.

    Enter Messenger.

MESSENGER
My lord, your brother John is ta'en in flight,
And brought with armèd men back to Messina.

BENEDICK Think not on him till to-morrow. I'll devise
thee brave punishments for him. Strike up, pipers!

                    Dance. [Exeunt.]

112 *double-dealer* married man, but also an unfaithful husband (a common
newly-wed joke)   119 *of* upon   121 *staff* rod of office, but also walking-
stick   121–22 *tipped with horn* (the usual reference to horns and cuckoldry)

A selection of books published by Penguin is listed on the following pages.

For a complete list of books available from Penguin in the United States, write to Dept. DG, Penguin Books, 299 Murray Hill Parkway, East Rutherford, New Jersey 07073.

For a complete list of books available from Penguin in Canada, write to Penguin Books Canada Limited, 2801 John Street, Markham, Ontario L3R 1B4.

The Complete Pelican
SHAKESPEARE

To fill the need for a convenient and authoritative one-volume edition, the thirty-eight books in the Pelican series have been brought together.

THE COMPLETE PELICAN SHAKESPEARE includes all the material contained in the separate volumes, together with a 50,000-word General Introduction and full bibliographies. It contains the first nineteen pages of the First Folio in reduced facsimile, five new drawings, and illustrated endpapers. 9¾ × 7³⁄₁₆ inches, 1520 pages.

SHAKESPEARE

Anthony Burgess

Bare entries in parish registers, a document or two, and a few legends and contemporary references make up the known life of William Shakespeare. Anthony Burgess has clothed these attractively with an extensive knowledge of Elizabethan and Jacobean England for this elaborately illustrated biography. The characters of the men Shakespeare knew, the influence of his life on his plays, and the stirring events that must have been in the minds of author, actors, and audience are engagingly described here by a writer who sees "Will" not as an ethereal bard but as a sensitive, sensual, and shrewd man from the provinces who turned his art to fortune in the most exciting years of England's history. "It was a touch of near genius to choose Mr. Burgess to write the text for a richly illustrated life of Shakespeare, for his wonderfully well-stocked mind and essentially wayward spirit are just right for summoning up an apparition of the bard which is more convincing than most"—David Holloway, *London Daily Telegraph*. With 48 plates in color and nearly 100 black-and-white illustrations.

THE AGE OF
SHAKESPEARE

Edited by Boris Ford

This second volume of *The Pelican Guide to English Literature* covers the Elizabethan literary renaissance. An extensive survey of Elizabethan literature and society is followed by a number of essays that consider in detail the work and importance of dramatists, poets, and prose writers—Cyril Tourneur, George Chapman, Thomas Middleton, Samuel Daniel, Sir Walter Ralegh, and Francis Bacon, among many others. The emphasis is on the dramatists, and five of the essays are devoted to Shakespeare's plays alone. An appendix gives short biographies of authors and lists critical commentaries, books for further study and reference, and standard editions of Elizabethan works. Boris Ford is Professor of Education and Dean of the School of Cultural and Community Studies at the University of Sussex, England.

INTRODUCING SHAKESPEARE
Third Edition

G. B. Harrison

Now a classic, this volume has been the best popular introduction to Shakespeare for over thirty years. Dr. G. B. Harrison discusses first Shakespeare's legend and then his tantalizingly ill-recorded life. Harrison describes the Elizabethan playhouse (with the help of a set of graphic reconstructions) and examines the effect of its complicated structure on the plays themselves. It is in the chapter on the Lord Chamberlain's Players that Shakespeare and his associates are most clearly seen against their background of theatrical rivalry, literary piracy, the closing of the playhouses because of the plague, the famous performance of *Richard II* in support of the Earl of Essex, and the fire that finally destroyed the Globe Theater.

PENGUIN ENGLISH LIBRARY

The Penguin English Library Series reproduces, in convenient but authoritative editions, many of the greatest classics in English literature from Elizabethan times through the nineteenth century. Each volume is introduced by a critical essay, enhancing the understanding and enjoyment of the work for the student and general reader alike. A few selections from the list of more than one hundred titles follow:

BEN JONSON: THREE COMEDIES
Edited by Michael Jamieson
VOLPONE, THE ALCHEMIST, BARTHOLOMEW FAIR

JOHN WEBSTER: THREE PLAYS
Edited by D. C. Gunby
THE WHITE DEVIL, THE DUCHESS OF MALFI,
THE DEVIL'S LAW-CASE

THREE JACOBEAN TRAGEDIES
Edited by Gāmini Salgādo
THE REVENGER'S TRAGEDY, *Cyril Tourneur*
THE WHITE DEVIL, *John Webster*
THE CHANGELING, *Thomas Middleton and William Rowley*

FOUR JACOBEAN CITY COMEDIES
Edited by Gāmini Salgādo
THE DUTCH COURTESAN, *John Marston*
A MAD WORLD, MY MASTERS, *Thomas Middleton*
THE DEVIL IS AN ASS, *Ben Jonson*
A NEW WAY TO PAY OLD DEBTS, *Philip Massinger*

THREE RESTORATION COMEDIES
Edited by Gāmini Salgādo
THE MAN OF MODE, *George Etherege*
THE COUNTRY WIFE, *William Wycherley*
LOVE FOR LOVE, *William Congreve*

Also works by Jane Austen, Charlotte Brontë, Emily Brontë, John Bunyan, Samuel Butler, Wilkie Collins, Daniel Defoe, Charles Dickens, George Eliot, Henry Fielding, Elizabeth Gaskell, Thomas Malory, Herman Melville, Edgar Allan Poe, Tobias Smollett, Laurence Sterne, Jonathan Swift, William Makepeace Thackeray, Anthony Trollope, Mark Twain, and others

PLAYS BY BERNARD SHAW

ANDROCLES AND THE LION

THE APPLE CART

ARMS AND THE MAN

BACK TO METHUSELAH

CAESAR AND CLEOPATRA

CANDIDA

THE DEVIL'S DISCIPLE

THE DOCTOR'S DILEMMA

HEARTBREAK HOUSE

MAJOR BARBARA

MAN AND SUPERMAN

THE MILLIONAIRESS

PLAYS UNPLEASANT
(WIDOWERS' HOUSES, THE PHILANDERER,
MRS WARREN'S PROFESSION)

PYGMALION

SAINT JOAN

SELECTED ONE ACT PLAYS
(THE SHEWING-UP OF BLANCO POSNET,
HOW HE LIED TO HER HUSBAND, O'FLAHERTY V.C.,
THE INCA OF PERUSALEM, ANNAJANSKA, VILLAGE WOOING,
THE DARK LADY OF THE SONNETS, OVERRULED,
GREAT CATHERINE, AUGUSTUS DOES HIS BIT,
THE SIX OF CALAIS)

THE VIKING PORTABLE LIBRARY

In single volumes, The Viking Portable Library has gathered the very best work of individual authors or works of a period of literary history, writings that otherwise are scattered in a number of separate books. These are not condensed versions, but rather selected masterworks assembled and introduced with critical essays by distinguished authorities. Over fifty volumes of The Viking Portable Library are now in print in paperback, making the cream of ancient and modern Western writing available to bring pleasure and instruction to the student and the general reader. An assortment of subjects follows:

PENGUIN CLASSICS

The Penguin Classics, the earliest and most varied series of world masterpieces to be published in paperback, began in 1946 with E. V. Rieu's now famous translation of *The Odyssey*. Since then the series has commanded the unqualified respect of scholars and teachers throughout the English-speaking world. It now includes more than three hundred volumes, and the number increases yearly. In them, the great writings of all ages and civilizations are rendered into vivid, living English that captures both the spirit and the content of the original. Each volume begins with an introductory essay, and most contain notes, maps, glossaries, or other material to assist the reader in appreciating the work fully. Some volumes available include: